LUSCINIA

Borgo Press Books by BRIAN STABLEFORD

LUSCINIA

A ROMANCE OF NIGHTINGALES AND ROSES

by

Brian Stableford

THE BORGO PRESS

An Imprint of Wildside Press LLC

MMX

CONTENTS

DEDICATION

FOR LINDA AND ELAINE

AUTHOR'S NOTE

The story briefly summarized by the protagonist in the second chapter of Part One is *Luscignole* (1892) by Catulle Mendès; an English translation can be found in the collection *Number 57*. Louis Aragon's *Le Con d'Irène* was originally published in 1927 under the pseudonym Albert de Routisie; it was reprinted in the 1950s under the author's real name and has been in print ever since.

PROLOGUE

THE CONNOISSEUR

It was about ten-thirty when the doorbell rang. I assumed that it was the postman delivering a book I'd ordered from Amazon, although that didn't make it any less annoying that I had to abandon the computer and make the long trek along the hallway from the back room that I called my "study".

It wasn't the postman. It was a balding man in his fifties in a smart grey suit, carrying a black leather briefcase. He didn't look like a salesman—more like a solicitor. I must have assumed an expression suspended somewhere between suspicion and loathing, but he didn't flinch. Instead, he looked me up and down, inquisitively, while I inspected the grey Volvo parked in my driveway. I'm not the sharpest tool in the box when it comes to reading expressions, but I thought I saw hints of uncertainty and disappointment in his, as if he weren't certain that I could be the person he'd been expecting to find, and would really rather that I wasn't.

"Crispin Ellsworth?" he asked, dispelling any hope and suspicion I might have had that he had the wrong address.

"I don't give out information on the doorstep," I said, abruptly.

"Very wise, I'm sure, Mr. Ellsworth," he said, mildly. He whipped a business card out of his wallet with practiced ease and handed it to me. "I'm J. K. Priestley," he went on—unnecessarily, since the name J. K. PRIESTLEY was inscribed on the card, above

the similarly-capitalized legend IMAGISTIC ENTERPRISES—
"I'm an exhibition curator. I work on a freelance basis, but in the
past I've been commissioned by the V&A, the Tate Modern and do-
zens of other institutions in and out of London. You can find my CV
on my website, if you're interested. You might well have seen some
of my work."

"I don't get into London much," I muttered. "What on earth do
you want with me?"

"I'm organizing an exhibition of the work of Devon Curtin at a
gallery in Piccadilly—not the Academy, alas, but quite nearby."

"Never heard of him." For a moment, I actually thought that he
might have the wrong Crispin Ellsworth, although it's not the kind
of name that lends itself readily to identity confusion.

The balding man elevated his head slightly in order to look me
in the eye—causing me to look away reflexively—and raised a
quizzical eyebrow. His lips sketched the beginnings of a sneer,
which he immediately checked. I assumed that he thought I that was
lying, but I wasn't, even though what I'd said was direly mistaken.
When acute anguish eventually fades into tranquil despair, the fading process has to bury certain memories. I really had buried the
name along with the song that Devon Curtin had set in my soul.

"I'm quite sure that you have heard of him, Mr. Ellsworth,"
Priestley retorted, twisting the unformed sneer into a parody of an
amiable smile, "although you might have to cast your mind back
twenty years, if you haven't been keeping up to date with recent developments in the relevant field." His tone implied that I really
ought to have been keeping up, and that he was surprised as well as
disappointed that I hadn't.

I was still nonplussed, but I did try to cast my mind back twenty
years, and a faint bell did ring somewhere in the depths of my memory. The note chimed by the cracked bell was "murder". For the
moment, though, I couldn't quite remember whether Devon Curtin
had been the victim or the perpetrator, or the particular circumstances of the crime.

"June the twenty-second will be the twentieth anniversary of his
death," the balding man offered, attempting to tease rather than in-
form. "We're planning a commemorative exhibition of his work.

I'm surprised you haven't heard—since we made the official announcement a week ago, we've been trying to generate as much buzz as possible, and I rather thought we'd succeeded, given the reaction on the Web. The exhibition will consist mostly of flash and photographs from his collection, of course, but we're attempting to recruit as many live models as we can. There are two pieces of work, in particular, that we'd be extremely interested in exhibiting in the flesh, although we do appreciate that your case is particularly problematic, in that the work extends over two individuals. We haven't located the former Miss Selvedge yet, and I'm hoping that you might be able to help with that."

Oddly enough—perhaps crazily—the name Selvedge didn't immediately ring a bell either, because Claire was indelibly enshrined in my memory as "Claire", her detached surname having long become a vestigial appendix of no interest. Again, I wondered confusedly whether he'd got the wrong Crispin Ellsworth, or whether I'd somehow developed amnesia without being aware of it. My confused gaze must have flickered in every possible direction while avoiding his face, and I must have looked almost demented. The garden looked even more like a jungle than usual, even though the growing season hadn't really got under way yet. All the bushes alongside the drive had long been drowned by bindweed, transfigured into sinister burial-mounds.

Then it clicked. This was about Luscinia.

Devon Curtin, murder victim. Devon Curtin, anonymous when I met him—when Claire and I met him—in The Artificial Paradise, but belatedly equipped with a name by the subsequent newspaper reports, and one dismally off-hand police interview. Devon Curtin, flash artist—flash, in this instance, being the quasi-technical term for copyrighted designs produced by tattooists who liked to think of themselves as Artists with a capital "A." Devon Curtin, author of Luscinia.

Reflexively, my right arm came away from my side, where it had been hanging loosely. Even though I wasn't making eye contact, I was conscious of the fact that J. K. Priestley's eyes immediately went to the area I'd exposed, with an inexplicable avidity. I realized, with a slight shock of surprise, that he knew that Luscinia was there, although he couldn't know her name. I cursed myself for the shock—of course he knew that she was there; why else would he have come to see me?

Although it was a sunny day, April Fool's Day was still a week away and the study was still bracingly cold in the mornings, because I'd never got around to installing central heating in the house I'd paid so dear to keep. In consequence, I was wearing a thick dark green pullover over a white shirt: a barrier impenetrable by the human eye. J. K. Priestley couldn't see a thing, and there was no way for him to imagine exactly what lay beneath the barrier, but that wasn't stopping his imagination working. I wondered if women felt the way that I was feeling when men stared at the clothing concealing their breasts.

He must have realized that I was aware of his futile stare, because he said: "Forgive me. Curating isn't just a job, you know—it's more a vocation. I like to think of myself as a connoisseur, in this instance above all. I find Devon Curtin's work utterly fascinating, and I'm as intrigued by the mystery of his unseen work as the most diehard of fans of his designs."

The full implication of what he wanted from me hit me then, like an unexpected jab in the ribs. "Oh shit," I said. "You want me to stand in an exhibition hall in Piccadilly, naked to the waist, showing off my bloody tattoo? No way. Absolutely not."

I felt ruffled feathers; a feeble flutter of wings; her long dormancy was already ended. It was only a matter of time before the song resumed, by day as by night.

I tried to put the sensation out of my soul and the idea out of my head, but it was futile.

"Actually," said the self-described connoisseur, his voice still as mild as milk, "standing wasn't what we had in mind. You'd be paid, of course—quite generously, given the importance of the work. Not that we're in a position at present to judge its artistic merits, alas—but it's become all the more important by virtue of the mystery attached to it. Given that it might prove to be a significant attraction, thanks to the Web buzz, we'd be prepared to pay quite handsomely—always provided that we can locate your...partner."

"Whose reaction, I'm sure, would be exactly the same as mine," I told him, my voice full of the conviction that comes from voicing an immediate reaction, without the luxury of the kinds of doubt that analytical thought engenders. "Give it up, Mr. Priestley. There's not a snowball's chance in hell." I made as if to shut the door in his face.

He didn't move or flinch. I hesitated.

"The problem is exaggerated, Mr. Ellsworth," the curator observed, pronouncing his words with a certain calculated emphasis, "by the fact that we don't have a photograph of the piece. Devon had to wait until his pieces were properly settled, the inflammation had eased and the scabs had peeled off before photographing his work. Because yours was the last major piece he completed before his death, he never got the opportunity to make a record for his archive. If you won't consider exhibiting the piece in the flesh, perhaps you'd at least allow us to arrange for photographs to be taken? Once we've located the other half of the work, that is."

"I haven't the slightest idea where Claire is now—or what her surname might be nowadays, assuming that she's been married in the interim."

"That does make the search more difficult," Priestley confessed. "We were hoping—and my associate was rather expecting—that both of you might contact us off your own bat when you heard about the exhibition, but it seems that we've assumed too much in thinking that the news was bound to reach you. We've had to put a detective agency on the job. They'll find The Rose, I'm sure."

"Is that how you found me? A detective agency?"

"It wasn't necessary in your case, once I had discovered your name. That was the difficult part—the record that Melanie made on the night in question had been taken by the police as evidence, and it was the Devil's own job to get a look at it, even after all this time, given that the case was never closed. Once we had the name, though, a simple internet search sufficed. The agency that provides you with translation work has a directory of its employees on its website, showing off their degrees and vocational qualifications— the CVs are brief, but adequate for identification purposes. Your address was easy to locate once we had identified your home town— you're not even ex-directory. As you observed just now, the fact that women's surnames routinely change over time makes it more difficult to locate them by that means; we had the same problem with The Goddess."

The name triggered another wisp of memory. "You can learn a lot from Lydia," I murmured, talking to myself rather than to my unexpected visitor—but he heard me. At least, he heard the final syllables.

"If you have any information about the present whereabouts of The Goddess," the freelance curator was quick to put in, "I'd be very grateful to receive it."

"Not a damn thing," I said. "But you definitely have photographs of her—I remember looking at a set of them while the needle was grinding into me, singing like a hornet all the while. I don't even know her real name. I just remember the tattooist referring to her, flippantly, as Lydia, and then having to explain the reference to the Groucho Marx song. I'd never heard it at the time, but I have since. It always strikes a chord." I was just trailing off when another thought occurred to me. "He was shot dead in his studio," I recalled. "You said the case was never closed—they never figured out who did it?"

"The case is still open," Priestley confirmed. "It wasn't Armina who shot him, if that's the thought that just crossed your mind."

The silence of another bell failing to ring seemed oddly conspicuous. "Who the hell is Armina?" I demanded, a trifle intemperately. I had the sensation that he was playing with me, hoping to get me hooked and draw me in, so that he could wear down my automatic resistance to his proposition.

"The Goddess—the woman that Devon sometimes referred to, with altogether undue contempt, as Lydia. Her real name was—and still may be, if she hasn't remarried or died—Armina Holliman."

I was still unable to recall more than the vaguest memory of the images I'd seen on the wall of the "studio" in The Artificial Paradise, but I was perfectly sure that Armina Holliman, entitled The Goddess in her role as a work of art, when she wasn't being dismissively nicknamed Lydia, wasn't going to get away with being naked to the waist if she were to show off her examples of Devon Curtin's patient labors. I could see why the curator thought that recruiting a few live models for his exhibition might increase attendance, even though the passage of time would mean that not one of them could be under thirty-eight years of age, and The Goddess probably bore more resemblance to a Mother Goddess than a Sex Goddess nowadays.

I remembered then what Priestley had said about standing not being what he had in mind for the exhibition of my own "piece".

"Absolutely no way," I repeated. "I don't care how famous Devon Curtin has become in whatever connoisseur circles you orbit in, Mr. Priestley, or how fashionable tattoos might have recently become as works of Modern Art with a capital M and a capital A. Mine isn't coming out to play, even for a set of dirty photographs. Forget it. You've wasted your time—you should have rung instead of driving all the way out from London, and saved yourself the trip."

"I only work in London," he said. "I live in Twyford, so I only had to make a small detour on my way in. I thought it would be better to make the approach in person."

"Well, it wasn't," I said firmly.

This time, I actually moved the door; this time, he actually put out his hand to prevent it from closing. Neither gesture was particularly insistent. I allowed him to stop me shutting him out, but it was only a truce—just a matter of giving him time to release a parting shot.

"I'm very sorry that you feel that way, Mr. Ellsworth," he said. "I hope you'll continue to think the matter over. As I said, there would be a generous fee. You have my card; if you change your mind, please get in touch. And if you don't, I hope you'll come to see the exhibition when it opens. I'll send you a brochure. I'm sorry to have troubled you."

He stepped back, giving me tacit permission to close the door. I closed it.

His parting shot hadn't been quite as inoffensive as it seemed. He *had* troubled me. Even as I turned to go back along the corridor, I was very much aware that what had happened twenty years ago was only a tiny part of the story, so far as I was concerned. The rest of it couldn't possibly be known to J. K. Priestley, so he couldn't possibly have suspected exactly how much he might have troubled me, but there was far more to Luscinia, so far as my own psyche was concerned, than even Devon Curtin or my once-beloved Claire could ever have suspected.

Or could they?

Devon Curtin and his receptionist-cum-assistant had talked about the origins of tattooing as a particular kind of magic, and Curtin must have had plenty of experience observing the relationships conjured up by the symbolism of people's chosen tattoos. As for Claire, pure bright Claire, brief as our acquaintance had turned out to be, might she not have believed that she had touched me as sensitively as I believed that I had touched her? Might she not think of Luscinia every time her fingers strayed over her blood-stained rose or her sky-blue eyes caught a glimpse of it in the bathroom mirror? Wasn't it stranger, in a way, that for such a long time I was so easily able to hear Luscinia's song *without* immediately thinking of the Rose for which she was supposedly dying, for whose color she was supposedly yielding up her soul?

Luscinia had been dying for a long time, but had never died, even though her song had faded away as my life had become less acutely painful, settling into a dull petrifaction. I had always known that she wasn't dead, and that her agony might one day flare up again, but I had grown complacent in my dullness, in my stony emotional silence. Blotting out the memory of the Rose—or, at least, the mental reflex that associated the image of the bird and the image of the flower—had been one aspect of the fading of the song.

Even as I sat down at my keyboard, I knew that the song was going to become shrill again, as well as plaintive. How could it not? It didn't matter whether I appeared in J. K. Priestley's accursed exhibition or not; the mere fact that he had turned up on my doorstep to remind me of the buried past would be sufficient. No matter how carefully the mask of my selective amnesia had been applied by my unconscious mind, it was torn now, and the memories would all come welling up through the rent in the fabric, like pus from a bursting boil. The process had hardly begun, but the damage was already done. From now on, it would be a matter of slow but irresistible pressure—and maybe not so slow, if Priestley's visit turned out to be the first domino in a sequence.

"Welcome back, St. Luscinia," I whispered, bitterly, talking entirely to myself. My right hand suddenly began to quiver, as if fearfully—as if there were something that my miseducated autonomic nervous system didn't want me to touch. It wasn't the keyboard toward which I had automatically reached out; it was a connection far more intimate than that.

Luscinia was about to start singing again, and struggling. What if...?

I refused to finish the thought, intent on remaining in denial, even though I knew that it was hopeless.

I forced my fingers down on to the keyboard, and forced my eyes to focus on the screen in front of me. Then, deliberately, I looked at the second screen, where the text I was in the process of translating was displayed, and began the process of making connections, organizing the flow from French to English. There was nothing in the world, I thought, more likely to quell uneasy memories than translating a dull-as-ditchwater business software manual from French into English. There was nowhere further away from the art and magic of a tattooist's parlor than the abstract jargonized world of *logiciels*, *procigiels* and *systèmes d'exploitation*.

If only I'd been able to absorb myself fully in the work, I might indeed have managed to get away. I wasn't, of course. The memories kept coming back regardless—and the process became increasingly insistent, prolific and rapid, far too hectic for immediate organization and comprehension, but all the more overwhelming for exactly that reason.

When I stopped for lunch I didn't even try to go back to work thereafter, and I knew by noon that I was due for a sleepless night of Luscinian song.

I picked up the phone once, to call Karen, but I put it down again before dialing. What could I say to her? She knew the history of the tattoo, of course—she'd been fascinated by it when she was a little girl, when she had often asked to see it when I tucked her into bed, and I had shown it to her, unbuttoning my shirt as if sharing a secret that was ours alone—but she only knew the story as a set of facts. I'd never told her about the obsessive dreams, let alone the other connections Luscinia had in my memory and imagination.

Anyway, I had to get things straight in my own mind first. Until I had restored the whole business to my conscious mind, I couldn't even begin to explain it to someone else, even my own daughter—and I did have to restore it. I knew that. I had to restore it, because there was no way that closing the door on the connoisseur of Devon Curtin's Art was going to be the end of the matter. It was only the beginning—and the exhibition, it seemed, was still three months away.

"Absolutely no way," I repeated, and meant it—but even as I said it, I was imagining myself already naked, already lying prone on top of some strange pale ghost, looking into her sky-pure eyes, sensing the amazing texture of her skin and the flesh within it, exploring the secrets of her inner being, while the thorn-briar tore at Luscinia's ready flesh, and the life-blood ran out of her...out of me...to fall like gentle rain on the petals of a white rose, in futile sacrifice.

I remembered the refrain of Luscinia's song: the beautiful, melodic, plaintive song. And I remembered what I'd made of it, and what it had made of me.

The last thing I wanted was to turn back the clock, but nothing I could do could prevent time itself running backwards, now the switch had been thrown and the universe had changed gear.

Unable to help it, I wondered what it would be like to see Claire again, after all these years, in the flesh...and to touch her again, with all the consciousness of which flesh is capable, in a way that I hadn't touched anyone at all for thirteen years, except in my dreams. There is, alas, an ineradicable streak of petty romance in all of us. Some memories can never be entirely forgotten, or entirely tarnished, even if clever amnesia sets them aside, and dulls their brightness.

Then, and only then, did I hear the song of the Nightingale rising up in the daylight, and feel a twinge of actual physical pain beneath my arm, as I was cruelly dragged from the tranquil tedium of my almost-contented despair toward something resembling ominous excitement and horrid hope.

PART ONE

MAKING CONNECTIONS

CHAPTER ONE

The Es we'd taken at the eve-of-results party weren't responsible for what happened, although Claire subsequently tried to put the blame on them. If ecstasy had anything to do with it, it was entirely natural ecstasy—the ecstasy of connection, of physical congress, of connubial bliss. And even if the ecstasy—the chemical as well as the natural—had played a part in the brief drama of our head-over-heels infatuation, it certainly wasn't the fact that we were high that impelled us into The Artificial Paradise on that cool spring afternoon, after the night when we'd danced and made love.

I don't say "made love" for euphemistic reasons—as will be observed soon enough, I have no intention of being excessively coy in matters of language, because I couldn't bring out the full meaning of the story if I were—but because that was exactly how I thought of it at the time. Knowing now how brief our encounter was, there's a temptation to be dismissive of the feelings associated with it, but that wouldn't be right. I was utterly and completely in love, and I think we both felt that, in our different ways.

It was the first time for both of us, and that made it a big deal, especially in view of my problems, and even more especially in view of the fact that we were both twenty going on twenty-one—which was deemed to be hellishly late to lose one's virginity, in the early 1990s—but I don't believe, even now, that it was just the effect of it being the first time, or of the first time having been so long delayed. It *was* love, in the full sense of the word, even though it turned out to be so evanescent.

I won't speak for Claire, even though I had my suspicions about the reasons why she had conserved her virginity so long, but I need to explain about myself, because the story doesn't make sense otherwise. It wasn't for lack of trying that I'd never got that far before, nor for the lack of anything else; I preferred to think of it as a kind of superfluity, or super-sensitivity, which made me a better man rather than an incompetent one.

"Some psychologists call it a touch taboo," the psychotherapist attached to the university counseling service explained to me, when I finally plucked up the courage to explain the difficulty to him, "but that's not quite the right term. 'Taboo' makes it sound as if it's socially-induced, a matter of over-controlled upbringing, but now we understand a little better what's actually involved, we're pretty sure that it's neurological in origin. It's an Asperger's trait. Have you heard of Asperger's Syndrome?"

I hadn't. Hardly anyone had in those days—except for trendy psychotherapists who liked to keep abreast of the latest literature.

"Well, we think it arises as an occasional side-effect of the neural transformation that occurs in the brains of male embryos in the seventh month of development. That's when male brains are differentiated from female brains in terms of their subtle neural architecture—the ultimate source of the differences between stereotyped male behavior and stereotyped female behavior that license such sayings as 'Men are from Mars, women are from Venus.'

"There's a whole cluster of different behavioral manifestations, which routinely differ idiosyncratically, and there's a wide spectrum of differences within each sex, but in broad terms, most of the behaviors we think of as typically male are Asperger's traits. Others, of course, really are socially induced—swaggering macho behavior, for instance, seems to be mainly determined by social pressures; it's not one of the things that tends to be further exaggerated when the neurological disposition becomes more extreme.

"When some or all of the Asperger's traits are exaggerated to extremes at which they prevent normal social functioning, the result is autism, but there's a wide spectrum between autism and commonplace male behavior. Mild exaggerations of the less obvious traits routinely pass unnoticed, or are dismissed as trivial quirks of personality. You're obviously not far displaced along the spectrum in other respects—given that you're studying French I assume that you're not a secret mathematical prodigy, and that you're not incapable of understanding wordplay—but you do exhibit the key indicator that encourages the diagnosis."

He paused for dramatic effect, and I had to ask: "What's that?"

"An innate reluctance to make eye contact. Most people make eye contact naturally; it's what the ANS—the autonomic nervous system—leads them to do, without their being conscious of it. You don't. In fact, your autonomic response is to avoid it. It's not that you can't make eye contact, but you have to make a conscious effort in order to do so, and maintain that consciousness in order to maintain the contact. The moment you relax, you automatically look away. Given what you've told me about your problems with physical contact, you have a parallel problem with touch. It's not that you're incapable of touching other people, or that you can't bear to be touched, but that you have to do it consciously, and maintain the consciousness—because otherwise, your ANS kicks in, and you automatically withdraw, or flinch."

"Shit." I said. "How do I get rid of it?"

"You don't. At least, not without long and disciplined biofeedback training, and perhaps not even then—I don't know of anyone who's tried. It's not as bad as it sounds. The mere fact that I've pointed it out will help, because this is one instance in which simply being conscious of a problem helps to alleviate it—consciousness being, as it were, the heart of the matter. Now that you know that you need to bring your consciousness to bear in order to combat and overcome the autonomic reflex, you'll find it easier to do. And you ought to bear in mind that the condition is only problematic in certain special circumstances. There are a lot of situations in which we don't want to touch other people, or be touched by them, and the contrary disposition—that of people who find it unusually easy to touch others or are unusually inclined to invite touch—can lead to social difficulties even more awkward than the ones you're complaining about. Let's face it, you wouldn't think of it as a problem at all if you hadn't reached the age where you were desperate to fondle girls. Leave sex out of the equation, and it's hardly a problem worth worrying about."

It *was* a problem worth worrying about, though, because I was desperate to get a girl—one would suffice, I thought—*into* the equation of my existence, which was becoming utterly miserable for lack of one. It was all very well for the shrink to sit there, bathing in smug self-satisfaction; he was probably married, but I was twenty years old, and still a virgin, not for lack of effort in the preliminary stages, but for the apparent lack of an ability to take the process all the way, because unwarranted hesitation and flinching led to confusion and anxiety, which led to virtual paralysis.

"Then again," the counselor went on, "the disposition has its compensating advantages. You might have to summon up all the reserves of your consciousness to get into the process of sex, and to get through it, but if and when you can—and I'm sure that you will, eventually—you'll probably find the experience extraordinarily intense, simply because you're hypersensitive to all the touch sensations involved. People who take to sex like ducks to water, who find the whole thing perfectly natural, probably can't imagine the kind of ultra-conscious sensation you'll experience."

I liked the *probably*, given that he looked like a duck-to-water kind of guy to me, who couldn't possibly know what he was talking about. Except that, as it turned out, he really did know what he was talking about, whether he'd ever been able to experience it for himself or not. He'd hit the nail right on the head, in fact. It was difficult for me to get started and to follow through—and there was no miraculous transformation after my visit to the shrink, which took place months before the post-finals party—but when I finally did contrive to go all the way, I really did go *all the way*, and maybe further than your common-or-garden duck-to-water stereotyped Martian ever bothers to go, even if he can.

When I made love to Claire, I *felt* it. I was conscious of every nuance and moment of it. I had to be. And I *loved* it. I loved every last sensation, especially the delicate ones that required a little extra consciousness, a little extra concentration. Later, I began to wonder what I was might be missing in compensation for what I was getting—what particular pleasurable sensations might emerge from the natural way of making love—but at the time, with the psychotherapist's observations and assurances still at the forefront of my mind, as they had to be, I felt *blessed*. I was in a heaven of my own: a heaven that seemed, at that moment, to be uniquely my own. The ecstasy was natural, or only very slightly chemically-assisted, but the consciousness that went with it was wholly and beautifully artificial.

And that, however absurd it might seem, was one of the reasons why the name of The Artificial Paradise struck a chord in my soul the following day. If Claire and I had gone to university in Southampton instead of Reading, so that the local tattoo parlor had been called Tattoo Magic instead of The Artificial Paradise, I'd probably have walked past it the next day without a second glance—but we hadn't, and it wasn't. As the shrink had correctly observed, my Asperger's traits certainly didn't include insensitivity to wordplay, and I stopped, not yet fully emerged from one Artificial Paradise, amused to be confronted by another.

The Artificial Paradise had formerly been a betting shop, which had closed in the face of already-growing competition from on-line gambling. In a university area, such competition is bound to be keen. Nowadays, the only place south of Watford where betting shops are still opening rather than closing is Hackney, where the computer-literate are still an alien species, but the establishment that attracted my attention was at the very forefront of the trend. Every other shop in the parade that had changed hands while I'd been at the university had become a fast food outlet, a mini-supermarket or a charity shop. Students tended to make abundant use of all three kinds of establishment. I knew that the tattoo business was thriving as never before, especially with respect to female customers, but I had been surprised to see The Artificial Paradise even so, sandwiched between Perfect Fried Chicken and Help the Aged. It had intrigued me, even though I'd never had any particular desire to embellish my meager biceps with snakes or spiders' webs. It had obviously intrigued Claire too, because rather than in spite of the fact that she was one of the few girls in her year not equipped with a minuscule monarch butterfly or sprightly primrose at the base of her spine or just beneath her shoulder.

I had been into the betting shop a couple of times, on Grand National Day and Derby Day, so I'd taken more notice than usual when the tattoo parlor appeared in its place, as if by magic—but the thought of actually going into it had never crossed my mind, until I walked past it hand-in-hand with pure, bright Claire, to whom I'd recently made mad, passionate love.

Everything seemed like a miracle of magical coincidence that day—including the startling fact that we'd been at the university for three years, in the same Faculty, studying subjects whose offices and seminar rooms were in parallel corridors one floor apart, but had somehow never met, or even noticed one another in the distance, until that prodigious evening when we had gone from being strangers to lovers in a matter of hours. The hand of fate seemed to be active in everything, and it seemed to be caressing us, with a consciousness that had utterly overwhelmed its habitual reticence.

Claire must surely have felt something of the same sort, else she would have pulled me back; in fact, she seemed as enthusiastic to follow fate's plan as I was. "If we do," she said, as the idea crossed both our minds in a single composite trajectory, "we have to do it properly. Something bold, not tiny. Something original, not picked off one of those pattern posters on the wall—like the photos, but not the same, not a *copy*."

The walls of the front section of the shop were decked with displays of samples—I didn't know enough then to think of them as "flash"—interspersed with photographs displaying more complicated designs. The photographs were captioned with titles like The Falling Angel, The King of Hearts, The Serpent Prince and The Tree of the Knowledge of Good and Evil, which might have seemed stupidly pretentious if we hadn't been in such a benevolent state of mind, but which seemed at the time to be romantic.

"Did you have something in mind?" I asked. I didn't even know, at that stage in our frantically hurried relationship, whether she could draw, so I didn't dare ask her whether she could come up with a design herself that we might present to the tattooist as a model to be reproduced.

"Something with meaning," she said. "Not mock-mystical meaning, like supposedly Kabbalistic symbols, but something with a story attached."

If I'd ever heard Groucho Marx sing "Lydia" I might have suggested Washington crossing the Delaware, but I hadn't. Unfortunately, our whirlwind mutual passion hadn't yet generated much in the way of a story; we had nothing of our own on which to hang a meaningful image. We didn't even have a special song. That was why I said: "Meaning is in the eye of the artist, not the weft of the canvas." I thought at the time that it sounded authentically intellectual, even deep. I was trying to impress, and Claire was eager to be impressed.

We went inside. It was four o'clock in the afternoon on a Tuesday in the middle of June; the parlor had been open since noon, but afternoons weren't peak time, even on auspicious days, and the place was empty of customers. The receptionist behind the counter in the front section was peering intently at her black-painted fingernails, obviously bored but still delaying the courtesy of looking up at us. I didn't mind that; I was in no hurry to meet her gaze. She seemed to be about our age, although it was difficult to be sure. She was abundantly made up around the eyes, and her hair was dyed jet black. She was wearing lots of ersatz silver jewelry and studded leather wristbands. Her glossy leopard-skin top had narrow shoulder-straps and was cut low in the front and back alike, thus leaving her arms, her shoulder-blades and an abundant cleavage exposed, in order to display the images imprinted on her pale skin: images of bats, skulls, pentacles and strange curlicues. I couldn't see her lower body, because the counter was in the way, but I automatically imagined sleek black leggings and shiny boots. She was pretty, in a fiercely assertive sort of way, but not as pretty—in my estimation—as soft, delicate, understated Claire.

"I'll need to see some ID," the receptionist said, when she eventually condescended to acknowledge our presence. She didn't bother to ask us what we wanted, presumably because it would have been superfluous, but she added: "A formality, of course, but we have to do it."

We both had student ID cards, which declared us to be over the age of majority, though not yet twenty-one. The receptionist took them off us, and laid them down on an open notebook that lay on the desktop inside the counter. There was also a larger red-bound ledger on the desktop, with some sort of bookmark protruding from its pages, an old-fashioned telephone, and a grey metal cashbox with a key in its lock. The only concession to modernity was a machine for printing credit card details on to duplicate receipts; everything else was way beyond its official use-by date.

"When would you like an appointment?" was the next question in the receptionist's script. She had picked up her ball-point pen in her left hand; the tip was hovering unsteadily over the open notebook. I got the impression that writing wasn't her forte.

"Now, if possible," I said, glancing toward the bead curtain protecting the silent back room. "If you're not too busy, that is."

There was a slight rustling sound, and I took a closer look at the curtain, trying to determine whether anyone was on the other side, peering through. I was unintimidated by the thought that someone— presumably the tattooist—might be sizing us up. Indeed, I was glad to be sized up, thinking for once in my life that my dimensions were entirely adequate, with Claire by my side.

"We don't usually take walk-ins," the receptionist said, unconvincingly. Then she paused. She had heard the rustling too; she was awaiting further developments.

Five seconds passed while nothing happened; we were all waiting for something, although two of us, at least, didn't quite know what. I looked around, in order to tear my eyes away from the curtain, but I wasn't about to meet the receptionist's brazen gaze.

The only furniture in the space before the counter was a sort of bench upholstered in red leather, long enough for four people to sit side-by-side if they weren't too fussy about elbow room, or for one person to lie down at full stretch. I assumed that people occasionally did have to lie down, their bottle having run dry while they were under the needle. I didn't think it would happen to me, on that particular day. I was in love, buoyed up by a unique euphoria—of more than one kind, although little presumably remained of the strictly chemical effects of the previous evening, save for a vague aftertaste.

Then I looked at Claire. She was four inches shorter than me, and slender in build. Her hair was blonde and her skin seemed very pale, but somehow slightly luminous. I'd heard mention of a "post-coital glow" and had always assumed that it must be a kind of blush, but now I wondered. In a dim light, she might have passed for a ghost, given her white cheesecloth blouse and pale grey skirt, but in the light—even the muted and slightly jaundiced indoor light of the tattoo parlor's reception area—she seemed bright and slightly dazzling, like an eager flame. She was smiling.

Eventually, the man to whom I was subsequently able to put the name of Devon Curtin emerged from the back room, parting the strands of the bead curtain with a gesture that sent rippling waves through its multicolored façade. He didn't look like an artist, let alone a genius. He looked like a mechanic. The oily stains on his denim jacket weren't blood, but they didn't offer a good impression, and his faded jeans seemed none too clean. He wore his hair long, but not elegantly so; it was clumped and uneven. He had no beard, but wasn't exactly clean-shaven either. His eyes were pale blue, like Claire's, although that seemed odd on him because his hair and his complexion were dark. When he spoke, however, his appearance seemed to change instantaneously. His voice was soft and musical, with an accent that sounded sufficiently upper-class to bring about an immediate category translocation.

"What can I do for you?" he asked, without introducing himself.

"We'd like something that links us together," I said. "Not matching, but complementary." His voice gave me confidence that he would know the difference between "complementary" and "complimentary" and wouldn't mistake one for the other.

"My pleasure," he said. "Did you have anything specific in mind?"

"We're open to suggestions," I said, evasively.

"Most people are," he replied, negligently, "but are you willing to abide by my artistic judgment? That's a different matter."

I hesitated. Even in those days, when I was young and foolish, I hesitated too often, as instinctively fearful of saying the wrong thing as I was as of touch and eye-contact. I didn't hate myself for it, though. "He who hesitates is rarely lost," I used to say, to others as well as to myself, "provided that he uses the interval of hesitation constructively." It sounds pompous now and probably did then, to everyone except me. It also sounds stupid, now that I know how nearly impossible it is to hesitate constructively.

"Yes," said Claire. "You're the artist, after all." She didn't mention the weft of the canvas, but I knew that she was consciously echoing my own pretentious sentiment.

"One whose greatness will one day be recognized," said Devon Curtin, perhaps displaying prescience, but probably just bragging.

"Do you have something specific in mind?" I asked.

"Yes," he said. "Something very specific. It'll take time, though, so if you have anything planned for this evening, you'll have to come back another day."

"May we know what it is before you start, or do you want us to trust you blindly?" I asked.

"You're the paying customers," he said. "I'll give you a discount, if you'll indulge my whim, but this isn't a hobby. If cost's a crucial factor, limiting the time you can buy, we'll have to give it a miss. I'll need four hours." His eyes flickered toward the tariff displayed on the wall behind the receptionist's head, which was bowed once again over her notebook, apparently studying the schedule mapped out there. My face must have fallen slightly, because he was quick to add: "The discount, in this instance, would be forty per cent. We take all major credit cards. You don't have to make up your mind before I've shown you what I have I mind."

He disappeared into the back room again, leaving the curtain jiggling like a swarm of rattlesnakes.

The receptionist looked up. "That's a good offer," she said. "You're lucky you came in when you did—his first appointment's not till nine, and his fingers must be itching. It'll probably be weeks before he has another time-slot of that length free. He's very much in demand now that the word's getting around, and things will only get more intense from now on."

I looked at Claire, seeking instruction. She looked back. No girl had ever looked at me like that before. None ever did again, although I wasn't to know that at the time. Then I got out my credit card, although I didn't offer it to the receptionist. I was signifying that I was ready, but I was still hesitating, just in case.

The man who subsequently turned out to be Devon Curtin reappeared, holding a sheet of cartridge paper, on which he'd sketched an image in pastels. There were two anonymous torsos, cut off at the neck and the waist, one male and one female. Curtin held the piece of paper so that the two torsos were horizontal, the male atop the female as if the truncated individuals were making love in the missionary position, although the male, while still apparently supporting himself on his invisible left elbow, as gentlemen are supposed to do, was reaching forward with his right arm, exposing his right side, while the female's left arm was thrown back, exposing her left side.

On the male's right side there was a small but detailed design depicting a rather undistinguished brown bird in the grip of a long thorny twig entwined about its body. The bird didn't seem to be struggling, although it didn't seem to be dead either—at least, not yet. One of the thorns, longer than the rest, was penetrating its flesh on the breast, about where the heart might be, and drops of blood that had apparently seeped from the wound were falling downwards, the stream bridging the narrow gap between the two human bodies. On the female's left side, the drops were falling on to a white, almost diaphanous flower, whose petals seemed as delicate as a butterfly's wing, staining the petals red.

I was a student who had just finished his final examinations, due to graduate with a B.A. in French in a matter of weeks if the results turned out as hoped and expected. I thought highly of my intellect and understanding; I thought I had an exceedingly good grasp of the principles of symbolism. I knew that French symbolists often encoded semen as blood, and routinely used floral and avian imagery to represent aspects of sexual intercourse and desire. I thought that I understood exactly what that image implied, and exactly why it might suit an amorous young couple who had asked for complementary designs. I thought I knew it all, and that very sense of complete understanding made me far more sympathetic than I might otherwise have been to a design that was, to say the least, a trifle bizarre and a trifle morbid—and whose execution, in spite of its relatively restricted size, threatened to be more than a little painful.

Again, though, I looked to Claire for instruction. I didn't want to speak for her.

"It's perfect," was her judgment. She was about to graduate too, exam results permitting; she was studying English, but probably thought that she understood symbolism at least as well as I did. She didn't seem to be afraid of the prospect of spending a long time under a buzzing, probing, stinging needle. That probably seemed a small price to pay for the sake of love, and permanent possession of something so out-of-the-ordinary as to be unique.

Ordinarily, I'd have been terrified, but at that moment, I was in love. The world had been turned upside down, and the problem my autonomic nervous system had with touch had been shamed and ridiculed. I handed the credit card to the receptionist, who slotted it into the machine before returning to her notebook and painstakingly transcribing our names from our ID cards. After a brief pause, the machine printed out a duplicate receipt; I added my signature and accepted my copy, along with our ID cards. I handed Claire's ID back to her and, now fully committed, asked the artist: "How do we proceed?"

"I'll need you both while I mark you up," said the tattooist. "You'll have to assume the position—only pretending, of course, like actors shooting a scene. You can keep your lower garments on. Then I can work on you one at a time—you first...what's your name?" He was talking to me.

"Cris," I said.

"Right, Cris. Phase one will take about two hours; then you can swap places." He looked at Claire. "What's your name?"

"Claire," she told him.

"Right, Claire. I'd prefer it if you could wait out here while I work on Cris, and *vice versa*. I don't like to be watched while I work, if it's okay with you. Melanie will take care of you when you're done, Cris, if you feel a little woozy. By the time Claire's finished, you'll be in a fit condition to see her home. Will you be able to come back in a week or so, when the inflammation has gone down, the scabs have come off and the ink has settled in? I need to take some photographs, for my archive. I won't put them up on the walls without your permission, though." He waved a negligent hand at The Falling Angel and The Tree of the Knowledge of Good and Evil, as if dismissing them as the follies of exhibitionists.

"No problem," I said, having no way of knowing that the shop would become a crime scene long before the appointed date.

We went into the back room. Claire didn't hesitate over the removal of her bra, or the resumption of a position almost identical to
the one we'd adopted only a few hours previously. I contrived to
keep my left elbow down while I stretched out my right arm. It
wasn't a pose I could have maintained for long without causing myself—and Claire too, in all likelihood—considerable discomfort, but
Devon Curtin was a dab hand with a magic marker. He didn't sketch
out the whole design, merely indicating a few key points with dots
and curved lines. Within two minutes, Claire was fully clad again
and back in the front section of the shop, while I arranged myself in
a comfortable position that would allow the artist to go to work.

It all seemed to have happened very smoothly as well as very
quickly, with an entirely natural flow. It's only on looking back that
it doesn't seem natural at all, in any sense of the word—although I
certainly can't say that its artificiality was an effect of my own consciousness and sensitivity.

CHAPTER TWO

The first thing that Devon Curtin did was to bring out a pack of long, thin needles. "Do you mind if I insert these?" he said.

"Where?" I asked, uneasily.

"They're acupuncture needles," he explained. "If I place them correctly, they'll help to nullify the pain of the inking needle. They stimulate the release of endorphins, without themselves causing more than a slight sensation. It's quite safe. These are virgin needles, so there's no danger of infection—the inking needle will be brand new too, so there's no danger there either."

"I don't believe in acupuncture," I told him.

"That doesn't matter," he said. "I do."

Reluctantly, I gave him the go-ahead to inset the acupuncture needles. He didn't do so immediately. First he washed his hands and put a disposable plastic glove on his right hand. Then he bathed the area where the tattoo was intended to go with what was presumably water, although it didn't erase the markings he'd made. The "slight sensation" didn't seem to qualify as pain, but I was very conscious of its unpleasantness, as I would have been to any unfamiliar touch. I think I was already producing endorphins on my own, as part of a hormonal cocktail generated by circumstance, so it was probably my unusual neurological disposition that produced the sensation, but that didn't make it any easier to bear. When the inking needle first made contact with my skin, it stung hard enough to make me bite my lip and screw up my face, if not actually to squeal.

"A lot of my clients find that it helps to talk," said the tattooist. "Just say anything that comes into your head. I'll keep up my end of the conversation as best I can, but I'll probably get a little distracted.

It doesn't matter, though, if both of us end up talking drivel. Don't get into a confessional mode, though—it's not unknown for my clients to say more than they intended to in order to stave off the pain, and then they blame me for making their secrets leak out. Stick to intellectual matters, if you can. Tell me about your studies."

I tried, but it wasn't that easy; I'd just finished my studies, and put them away, at least for the time being. I didn't want to talk about all the stuff I'd been revising for weeks, or the exams in which I'd regurgitated it pell-mell. No matter how much I welcomed it, nor how much consciousness I brought to bear, the touch of the needle was difficult to bear.

He could see that I was having difficulties, not only with the stinging needle but the talking, and he was quick to take up the slack. Presumably, given the recent increase in the fashionability of his art and the situation of the shop in a university area, he had grown well used to needle-virgins, and had developed techniques for soothing their distress.

"In the beginning," he told me, "way back in the Paleolithic era, tattooing was a sort of magic. The archeological and paleontological evidence can only tell us so much, of course, but practicing tattooists get a feel for it that makes it easier to draw inferences—or jump to conclusions. All self-ornamentation was magic of a sort back then, but superficial ornamentation—fancy clothing, jewelry and face-paint—was essentially a matter of social magic, attempting to generate and command status and prestige among one's fellow men. Tattooing was a much more intimate matter of attempted self-transformation. Because the ink was beneath the skin, it was considered to add new attributes to the flesh and to the soul. It was intended to remake men internally—and I say 'men' rather than 'people' because there was always a sexual differentiation in such matters. Women, on average, went in more for superficial ornamentation, men for tattoos."

"Men are from Mars, women are from Venus," I managed to mumble.

"It's different now, of course," he went on. "Feminism changes everything, Nowadays, as many women want tattoos as men, maybe more. And who can blame them? Aren't women as much in need of self-transformation as men—or, if not actually in need, given that they're naturally more beautiful in body and mind, don't they at least have the same opportunities from which to benefit? Isn't it because they're naturally more beautiful, to look at and to touch, that they're capable of so much more in that regard? They have as much to gain from the magic as men."

"I don't believe in magic, either," I said.

"You might think that you don't," he countered, "but that's because your unbelief hasn't yet been tested. Smart people pride themselves on knowing that every roll of a roulette wheel is independent of the last—that the fact that red has come up four times in a row doesn't make it any more likely that black will come up next time. Even people who know that, however, and take great pride in knowing it, are still more likely by far to bet on black than red—because the knowledge, at the end of the day, no matter how secure and correct it may be, can't stand up against the neurological disposition to respect the pattern. It's the same with magic. Even when you know that it's not real, you can't resist seeing the patterns when they emerge, or threaten to emerge. At the end of the day, even the hardest skeptic in the world can't look a curse in the eye without an automatic impulse to flinch. If he can maintain his consciousness and his concentration, he can defy the impulse—but if he relaxes, even for a second, the primitive part of his brain takes over and he might as well be back in the Paleolithic, drenched in superstition."

I was listening as carefully as I could, although I wasn't able to concentrate fully on what he was saying. In a futile attempt to block out the pain, to which I could readily believe that I must be hypersensitive, because of my neurological disposition, I was staring at the wall in front of me, concentrating hard on the photographs and portraits collected there. Many were duplicates of those in the outer office—The Falling Angel was there again, colored wings trying desperately to catch an updraft, and the King of Hearts, who looked to me like a supermarket ad for St. Valentine's Day produce, along with The Tree of the Knowledge of Good and Evil, with sturdy trunk and expansive foliage, but they were supplemented by others, including The Golden Dragon, breathing flame and sulfurous smoke, The Book of Shadows, full of cryptic symbols, The Masque of the Red Death, a crimson orgy…and The Goddess.

In stark defiance of what the tattooist was saying, the great majority of the bodies on which the more elaborate tattoos were displayed seemed to be male, although The Goddess was a glaring exception. The Falling Angel was inscribed on a female body too, but its owner seemed to be heavily into body-building. The only truly feminine form, apart from The Goddess, bore a less ostentatious butterfly design whose caption was obscured. Perhaps, I thought, a larger proportion of the artist's female customers refused him permission to display their tattoos in his workshop, for reasons of delicacy.

The photographs were all close-ups, calculated to show off the tattoos. As in the sketch the tattooist had showed us, almost all of the bodies were truncated, devoid of heads and only showing lower bodies in order to display ankle tattoos. Only one set of prints showed an entire body, head to toe, and that was the set of images of The Goddess. The record of her body art required a whole series of pictures, all of them naked poses, shot from the front, the rear and both sides. A single glance, from a distance, might have left the impression that she had no tattoos, but was simply wearing a great deal of ornate jewelry; more concentrated attention quickly revealed, however, that all the jewelry was, in fact, mere imagery. There was a multilayered necklace, gem-studded plates over each nipple, bracelets and armbands, various thigh-bands and anklets, and what appeared to be a *cache-sexe* but was in fact a tattoo inscribed on a shaved pubis.

There was no false tiara, so the image could, in theory, have been cut off at the chin, but the photographer evidently considered that the face was a necessary element of the overall design. It was that of a woman apparently in her late twenties, with a Mediterranean complexion that might have been carved out of wood and polished. The lips were full and red, the eyes dark, the hair black. The "jewels" making up the various pieces of her imaginary outfit were of all shades, presumably mimicking sapphires, rubies, emeralds, diamonds and other precious and semi-precious stones to which I couldn't even put names. They were mounted in virtual silver and gold, arranged in intricate patterns and strings.

"Is that what you mean about women, being naturally more beautiful, also being capable of much more in the art of self-transformation?" I asked, pointing at The Goddess with my outstretched arm.

The tattooist followed the direction of my forefinger. "Perhaps not the best example," he said. "Client confidentiality forbids me to say anything about her, but I have to admit that she turned out to be less of a Goddess than we'd hoped or planned. Privately, I tend to think of her as Lydia, although the designs are nothing like those in the song?"

"What song?" I asked.

He sang the first verse and a chorus. "Groucho Marx," he said, "although I first heard it in a cover version by Stubby Kaye. There aren't any history lessons in the work you're looking at, and the *double entendres* are different in kind and implication, but the punch-line's still the same. 'You can learn a lot from Lydia.' It really does help, you know, if you try to do the talking, instead of just asking brief questions and supplying terse comments."

I didn't doubt that he was right, but I didn't seem to be getting used to the sensation of one needle drilling into my ribs while a dozen others vibrated in resonance as they stuck into me at odd angles. My eyes strayed from the photographs of the tattooist's work to a set of three portraits, all in monochrome. "I recognize Baudelaire," I said, proudly, "But who are the other two?"

"Oscar Wilde and Edgar Allan Poe. Most people recognize those two but not Baudelaire."

"I've just spent three years studying French," I told him, forcing myself to utter longer sentences. "I should have recognized Poe, though. Baudelaire translated him—helped his reputation in Europe no end."

"Maybe," the tattooist conceded. "On the other hand, maybe the spirit of Poe's genius entered into Baudelaire following his death, and it was Poe who helped Baudelaire become what he became. Poe was the greatest literary genius the world has ever seen, in terms of innovation and versatility, so far ahead of his time that he starved to death for lack of recognition, and his ghost has been haunting privileged individuals ever since, still hoping against hope to see that genius appreciated."

I was quick enough on the uptake to guess that he was being provocative, trying to make me think. He presumably figured that if I wouldn't or couldn't talk nineteen to the dozen, then I needed some mental labor to carry out. I figured that I ought to play along, for the sake of the burning sensation in my side, which still wasn't getting easier to bear, even though it didn't quite seem to qualify as agony.

"And after Baudelaire's death," I said, "the unquiet but benevolent spirit entered into Oscar Wilde—with maybe another less successful stop along the way. After Wilde, maybe H. P. Lovecraft, and after Lovecraft...well, who knows? Until it reached you, I suppose, having despaired of literary work and decided to explore pastures new. How does it feel to be haunted by such an obsessive ghost?"

"It has its pros and cons," he replied, off-handedly. "I do good work—but I'm uncomfortably aware of the fact that Chuck and Oscar both died at the age of forty-six, penniless, miserable and almost universally despised. Eddie didn't even make it that far before perishing of cruel neglect and grief."

"How old are you?" I asked.

"Forty-seven next birthday," he replied. "That's not until November, mind, so I might have a little time in hand yet."

"Let's hope so," I said. "What kind of bird is it that you're inscribing on my ribs?"

He hesitated, in a fashion that I recognized. "*Luscinia megarhynchos*," he said—and I got the impression that he would have stopped there had he not felt an obligation to explain. Very belatedly, he finally added: "A nightingale."

"I like *Luscinia*," I said, savoring the unfamiliar word. "It has a nice ring to it, reminiscent of 'luscious' and 'lucid'. I know a *conte cruel* about nightingales and needles. I think the original is by Catulle Mendès, but I've only heard it second-hand. Do you want to hear it?"

"Absolutely," he assured me, evidently thinking that it would loosen my tongue. "I don't think I've heard it, if it has needles in it instead of thorns."

"It's about an orphan girl," I told him, "whose guardian is a caretaker in a cathedral. He's famous because he knows the secret of making nightingales sing by day, but he won't tell anyone what it is. One night, when she can't sleep, the girl creeps up to the bell-tower where he's working, and sees him running red-hot needles into the eyes of captured nightingales. Once blind, they're unable to tell the difference between the darkness of night and daylight, so they sing by day."

The rhythm of his needling didn't change, but I was conscious of the fact that his body had changed position, as if he were wincing.

I plugged on. "Horrified by what she's seen, the little girl runs away, and becomes a vagabond. She has a fine singing voice, and makes a living by singing to passers-by. One day, a prince hears her, and is entranced. He has her abducted, sewn into a feathered costume, and placed in a cage in the forest where he rides and hunts. There she sings whenever he rides by, hoping that he might fall in love with her as she has fallen in love him, but he remains indifferent. Eventually, she loses hope, and her voice fades away. When she can no longer sing, she becomes useless, and is released from her cage. Expelled from the forest and forced back into vagabondage, she can no longer earn a living, and is on the brink of perishing when her former guardian, reduced to vagabondage himself, comes across her. He knows the secret of enabling birds to sing when nature can't prompt them, and is thus able to restore their fortunes, after a fashion."

"That's a good story, I suppose," Devon Curtin said, diplomatically, "but it's not one I'll be telling my clients. My needles are far more benign, and it wouldn't be in my interest to suggest otherwise. I wouldn't have asked you to tell it if I'd known how it was going to end—or how it was going to start, for that matter. I'd advise you not to think about it, if I thought it would do any good—but we both know what the effects are of telling someone not to think about something. It's probably too late now to tell you that there's an old legend about the nightingale singing with a thorn pressed to her breast in order to keep her awake, for fear of the vengeance of the slow worm whose eye she'd stolen because she only had one of her own—and it wouldn't be entirely relevant anyway, as it merely provided the spark for the story I had in mind. Nor would there be any point in telling you that the assumption that it's the female nightingale which sings—taken for granted by all story-tellers, it seems—eventually turned out to be mistaken. It's actually the males that sing."

"That certainly confuses the issue," I agreed, "but the stories are more significant than the reality. Don't worry about the possible after-effects of mine. A distraction is a distraction, even if it involves red-hot needles being run into nightingales' eyes. Anyway, the whole thing is an exercise in symbolism, just like your design—just like all your designs, if I'm reading them right: The Falling Angel, The Tree of Knowledge, The Book of Shadows and so on. Not surprising, really—all tattoos are symbolic; it's their sole *raison d'être*. You can call it magic if you like, but maybe the people of the Paleolithic Era were no more superstitious than we are. After all, we still go in for all sorts of self-ornamentation, without thinking that there's anything magical in its effects."

"You'd be surprised," he said, "how superstitious most of us still are, and how firm some people's belief in magic remains."

"But most people know that their superstitious rituals are just rituals—expressions in symbolism, and when people talk about magic nowadays they mostly do so metaphorically."

"Mostly, maybe," he agreed, a trifle dubiously, "but the opposition between the literal and the symbolic, or the real and the metaphorical, isn't a simple matter of either/or. There's always a continuum between the terms, and there's no way to tell exactly where one ends and the other begins. It's the same with science and magic."

"Not to mention genius and madness," I supplied. "Or fact and fiction."

"I'm not sure about those," he said, this time more than a little dubiously.

"But not love and hate," I was quick to put in. "No confusion there."

"Why not?" he said, feeding me the prompt so that I might feel free to ramble on.

"They're not really opposites," I said, "so they don't fit the pattern. It's wrong to think of them as opposites. The opposite of love is….well, indifference, the opposite of hate, serenity. There are continua between them, I suppose; love probably fades into indifference more easily than our hopes pretend—but so does hate into serenity, which is a brighter prospect."

I thought I was on a roll; I felt even more intoxicated then than I had earlier in the day, in spite of the waspish sting of the needle, perhaps because of the endorphins provoked by the acupuncture needles, or perhaps by virtue of mental resistance to the miniature hammer-drill. I was speaking as casually as I could, trying to offer every appearance of making it up as I went along, although I'd improvised parts of the speech long before and often repeated them. The argument seemed to have found its proper role at last: idle mock-philosophy voiced for the purpose of filling the ominous air with soothing sound and my stress-laden mind with a cloud of vaguely provocative thought. I felt proud of myself, although, in retrospect, I probably sounded like a fool to him.

"Fact and fiction aren't really opposites either," I decided. "The opposite of a fact is a downright lie, but fiction's more complicated."

"Genius and madness certainly aren't opposites," he told me, with the air of one who knew, "although there's certainly a continuum between them, and a great deal of confusion there."

"Are science and magic really opposites?" I queried, going with the flow.

"Definitely," he replied. "Science is the analysis and contrivance of causality, magic the analysis and contrivance of breaches in causality. Opposites for sure—and yet, there's a grey area between the two where causality bends and cracks, without actually fracturing. That's where free will creeps in."

"Or creeps out," I said, still feeling absurdly pleased with myself—all the more so because I was beginning to find the pain in my side bearable, and because time was passing by, every minute bringing me closer to the end…except that it wouldn't really be the end, if it was going to take a week for the residual inflammation to subside and the injury to heal.

That was an awkward thought, from which I immediately sought distraction. "Why a nightingale?" I asked, remembering how he'd hesitated before revealing the name by which *Luscinia megarhynchos* was commonly known. "I think I understand the symbolism of the bird, the blood and the flower, but why a nightingale, specifically? What story did you have in mind, if it wasn't mine? I know there's one by Hans Christian Andersen, but I've never read it."

"There's one by Oscar Wilde too," he said, a trifle reluctantly. "If you'd known that one, though, you'd probably have recognized his portrait. Poe's spirit was working overtime that day."

"And today," I said. "By the time you've finished with us, your next appointment will be due. You won't have much time for an evening meal—but I suppose there are advantages to being stuck in the middle of a row of takeaways."

"It's not exactly conducive to a healthy diet," the tattooist observed, "but what the hell—who wants to live forever?"

"I think Baudelaire might have been glad of the opportunity," I said. "And if Poe's spirit is still here, instead of crossing over to the other side, he obviously feels that there's still unfinished business to attend to. Personally, I'd quite like to have the chance of living forever—eventual boredom would be a small price to pay, in my estimation. After all, it wouldn't be compulsory to carry on forever, if it proved too difficult. The chance would be a fine thing, though, in case it didn't."

I realized, somewhat to my surprise, that I was relaxing even further, in spite of the persistent fire in my rib-cage. I wondered momentarily whether the experience might have put an end to my excessive touch-sensitivity for good, and whether I might now be better equipped to transform myself into a Don Juan, but that seemed a step too far, and I couldn't imagine that anyone who had Claire could possibly want anyone else. Cured or not, though, I seemed to have triumphed over the stress of the moment. The thorns surrounding my poor Luscinia might be tearing at my flesh as well as hers, frustrated because my own heart was out of reach even of the longest of them, but I was becoming increasingly capable of talking drivel by way of mental and emotional distraction, and that seemed to be no bad thing. I wasn't even afraid of lapsing into a confessional mode. I had no secrets to conceal.

"You have a point," Devon Curtin conceded, with respect to my discourse on the attractions of immortality.

"So have you," I countered, with a small giggle. "I can feel it boring into me, flooding me with color, as if it were red-hot and leaking its crimson wrath into my soul—but I'm supposed to be taking my mind off that, aren't I? Think cool, Cris, think smooth, think happy, think love. You twigged that Claire and I are freshly in love, of course, right away. Is that why you offered us your design?"

"To be perfectly honest," the tattooist told me, with a slight hint of regret, "It was the color and texture of your skin—perfectly pale, perfectly matched. Color is my business, you see, not love…but if you hadn't been freshly in love, you wouldn't have come in together, would you? And you wouldn't have been so ready to accept the offer. So, yes, in a way—it *was* the fact that you were in love that prompted me to make the offer, and guarantees the success of the work. I hope, sincerely and passionately, that your love will last a long time, and that you'll come together frequently in such a fashion as not merely to complete and display the work, but to lend it meaning through motion."

And sensitivity, I thought. *You don't know about the excessive sensitivity, but you'd be all the more delighted if you did.* I adopted a reflective tone to say, aloud: "Except that we won't be doing it in front of an audience, or even a video camera. Ours will be a private work of art—secret, even given that we won't be able to seen it ourselves, unless we position a mirror in exactly the right position and crane our necks."

"That doesn't matter," he assured me. "As I said before, a tattoo isn't mere surface, like a painting; its magic is within the flesh, deep down. The surface image is only part of it. The rest…well, I expect you'll find that out, in your own time and your own way. I hope you'll be glad of it, and proud of it. And I'll have the photographs, won't I? That's all I ever have, once the work is done, even if my clients become regulars. I have the photographs—the images—but it's my clients who have the actual tattoos within the substance of their flesh, to savor in all their true glory."

"You can learn a lot from Lydia," I repeated back to him, "but not as much as Lydia can learn from herself."

"Exactly so," he said, sounding genuinely pleased with the quip, which I really had improvised on the spot. "That's where the real learning takes place and the real magic unfolds. Only you can *feel* the transformation."

CHAPTER THREE

Melanie, the receptionist, padded the disfigured skin with cotton wool and wrapped a bandage round my torso to hold it in place, then helped me to put my shirt back on before I went back into the front office. Once I was sitting as comfortably as could be expected on the upholstered bench, she gave me a brief lecture.

"I'll give you some more cotton wool so that you can renew the dressing periodically. You can leave the tattoo undressed while you're naked to the waist, if that feels better, but dress it again before you put your shirt on. Don't take a bath or a shower for at least three days—stick to washing the other parts of your body. You'll be tempted to pick at the scabs, but you mustn't, even if they itch horribly. It's much better for the image if they're allowed to peel naturally, in their own time. The inks need to be integrated into the flesh—people don't realize how easy it is to spoil a design, and this is one that the Master won't want spoiling. He doesn't care about the everyday hackwork, but this is one of the ones he puts his heart and soul into. You were lucky to catch him with a gap in his schedule, although this is always a slow time of year. It stays light for far too long—there's something about winter darkness that encourages customers, and something about midsummer sunlight that deters them."

She had retreated behind her counter again by the time she'd finished, but I'd already seen the close-fitting black leggings and the shiny boots that completed her outfit. "Gothic gear is better suited by winter gloom than long summer twilights as well," I observed, "but you can still carry it off—especially in the annex to a tattoo parlor."

"Don't start chatting me up while your girl-friend's under the needle," she said. "It's unsporting."

I didn't bother protesting that I wasn't trying to chat her up. The needle had already started buzzing in the studio, and I listened briefly to its song, taking note of the fact that, although it didn't quite drown out the voices of the tattooist and his client, it blurred them sufficiently for their words to be indistinguishable. I felt a slight pang of regret at the thought that Claire hadn't been able to appreciate the heroism of my intellectual discourse, and wondered what she would find to say in order to distract herself from the threat of unbearable anguish.

I refrained from poking the bandage, but I probed a couple of the points from which the acupuncture needles had been withdrawn, curiously. I must have pulled a slight face, because the receptionist got up again and brought me two pills, along with a glass of water she'd poured from a bottle of Evian. I looked at them suspiciously.

"Ibuprofen," she said. "The pain sometimes begins to set in afterwards, once the excitement is all over. Take them—you'll be grateful."

"Thanks," I said, handing the glass back, still half-full, once I'd swallowed the pills. "Maybe I should carry on talking, to continue the distraction—as long as you won't think that I'm trying to chat you up."

"You won't be able to help it," she said, not sounding overly unhappy about the assumed inevitability. "You're male, and I'm gorgeous."

"I'm in love with Claire," I told her. "Really and truly."

"I know," she said. "It makes no difference. You can't escape your programming. It's different for women, of course. We're far more controlled, true mistresses of diffidence and single-mindedness."

It would have been ungentlemanly not to believe her, at least insofar as she was speaking for herself, so I made the effort. "Does… the Master manage to persuade many of his customers to let him indulge his artistic whims?" I asked.

"Not that many," she replied. "He has some special clients, who are only too eager to indulge him, but it's rare for him to make the kind of offer he made to you to people who wander in from the street. Your girl-friend has beautiful skin, though. I could see why he was interested. He knew he'd caught her at exactly the right moment, while she's transcending her customary shyness—perfect for the secret art."

"Secret art?" I queried.

"Didn't he bore you with all that? He sometimes rambles on about the transformation of the ancient magical art of tattooing by the invention and elaboration of clothing. He considers tattooing to be the highest of all the visual arts, of course, because of its intimacy. He's got a whole theory about human skin being far more than a mere backcloth, lending a particular kind of life to the artwork, and if he ever gets around to writing his book, there'll be several chapters about the effects of concealing tattoos beneath clothing, so that it becomes arcane, occult and secret. You probably haven't had time to think about it yet, but you're a work of art now—not just someone with a work of art printed on his outer surface, but a work of art *in yourself.* You've been transformed and transfigured—but no one else will be aware of it, while you swathe yourself in opaque clothing. It'll be entirely up to you to decide when to show yourself, to whom, and in what circumstances."

She was right; I hadn't had time to think about it yet—but I had time now, while I was waiting for Claire. So I thought about it, mostly aloud.

"*We*'re a work of art," I said. "The two of us. As a couple, we're a work of art. As a loving couple…while we're actually making love. Otherwise, we're just fragments, detached parts of something that only really exists when we're together. We've been transformed, but not individually. For the work of art to come together, to appear in all its glory, we need to be together—and not merely together, but in love. We can pose for photographs, but they'll only be the produce of pretence—essentially fake. Secret art—I like it. Not just hidden by clothing, but effectively invisible even when exposed, unless…I get it. I really do." I really thought I did.

My gaze had settled on her bare shoulders and arms. I wondered what images might still be concealed within her clothing, and whether she too had been the recipient of one of the artist's genuine endeavors. The thought must have been easily legible in my expression.

"That's part of the effect," she said. "Maybe worth a whole chapter. The designs that are exposed become tantalizing, seemingly offering hints as to what might be concealed in more intimate regions." Again, she seemed rather to relish the prospect and its possibilities. She didn't seem to me to be much of a model for diffidence, although the jury was still out on the charge of single-mindedness.

I thought about The Goddess then. If she dressed for everyday purposes in a buttoned-up blouse, with a long skirt or opaque tights to cover her ankle-bracelets, no one would have the slightest inkling about her "jewelry". Even if she permitted glimpses of her multilayered necklace and her anklets, who would be able to guess what her clothing might still conceal? Unless, of course, they too had lain on the tattooist's couch and stared at the photographs of her naked body.

"All the pictures on his wall," I said, reflectively, "were in super close-up, so that the people couldn't be identified—except for one set. One set showed a face, so that anyone encountering the face in question in the course of everyday life would know full well what her clothing was hiding."

"You mean Lydia," the receptionist said, with a slight curl of her lip.

"The Goddess," I said, chivalry demanding that I defend the unknown lady.

"Don't take too much notice of the titles," she said. "They're just for show. The Tree of the Knowledge of Good and Evil loses all its mystique when you find out that it's on the back of a jobbing gardener called Stan, the Masque of the Red Death is less impressive when you find out that its purpose is to disguise and ennoble *acne rosacea*, and The Goddess's divinity goes out of the window when you realize that she's just one more silly cunt—pardon my French."

Her final pseudo-apologetic phrase started a trivial train of thought, which meandered somewhat under the pressure of the pain I still felt and the ibuprofen that was beginning to take arms against it—but even trivial trains of thought can carry a good deal of intellectual freight.

As a student of French, I knew that the obscenity she'd used was echoed in French in the much milder and far more versatile *con*, as featured in Louis Aragon's classic pornographic novel *Le Con d'Irène*. A dog-eared copy of that novel had been passed around in my first year at the university, providing a much more entertaining opportunity for us all to increase our fluency in reading French prose than plowing through Balzac's *Illusions perdues*. It had been translated into English as *Irene's Cunt*. I knew that many French swearwords echo Anglo-Saxon equivalents, almost as if the French consider that there's something essentially obscene about the English language, and the English people themselves, but I also knew that the word in question had a more complex etymology, the Anglo-Saxon echo having been grafted on to a pre-existent noun, *con* or *conn*, derived from the verb *conduire*—to lead—and referring to the post occupied by the steersman of a vessel, as paralleled in English by the term "conning tower".

By virtue of that conflation, I knew, the title of Aragon's novel was actually a *double entendre*. As well as referring to the relevant part of Irène's anatomy, it also referred to the effect it had on the story's protagonist, becoming an object of obsession that took over his conscious life. In French, the noun was more frequently used to mean "fool" or "idiot" than anything authentically obscene, so the title could have been more appropriately translated as *Irene's Fool*. The related term *connerie* referred to a screw-up, and was only marginally offensive, although that had apparently been considered serious enough to have Sean Connery's name removed from the French advertisements for the first James Bond movie. That had always seemed grossly unfair to me, given the number of French words that started with the same combination of letters, including *connotation* as well as *connection*, *connaissance* and *connoisseur*. If every Frenchman had made the connection implied by the echo of "cunt" every time he heard a word beginning with *conn*, let alone *con*, his mind would have been focused on women's nether regions all day long…although that wasn't entirely impossible to believe of Frenchmen, or of stereotypical men in general, for whom the relevant anatomical feature could indeed be seen as the location of a metaphorical steersman.

I remembered then what the tattooist had said about being haunted by the spirit of Edgar Allan Poe: that it had its pros and cons. That was only one of the English phrases given new double-entendre potential by the French connection.

In my first year at university, the mere fact of the authorship of *Le Con d'Irène* had lent it an implication of surrealism that was easy enough to transfer, in the eye of the eager beholder, to other works of upmarket French porn, from Guillaume Apollinaire's *Les Onze mille verges* to Pauline Réage's *Histoire d'O*. Being students, of course, we all preferred upmarket French porn to *Playboy*, or pretended to. It probably colored the way we thought about women, and about sex, but as long as the coloration was surreal, it didn't seem to matter....

While I was following this train of thought, my pensive gaze settled on Melanie's face, although I didn't intend to meet her eyes, and only realized belatedly that she was staring back at me. When I did realize it, and immediately looked away, I must have blushed crimson, because she laughed.

"Told you so," she said. "Don't worry about it—the pain of the needle often makes people think they're horny. The stimulation is open to reinterpretation. Try not to think about it."

That instruction was even more futile now than when the Master had advised me not to think about the little girl's guardian running red-hot needles into the eyes of nightingales. The more I tried to change the mental subject, the more I kept being drawn back to words beginning with *conn*, and thence to Melanie's charms, and whatever secret art her clothing might conceal, and how the imagination of it might steer and guide male attention. I tried to think about Claire instead, and about how *claire* had a much wider range of meaning in French than its English equivalent *clear*, how its primary meaning was *bright*, especially in the context of weather, and how its association with cloudless skies also lent it an implication of purity...but I was all too well aware of Claire's steersmanship, and I couldn't focus, for the moment, on her brightness or her purity....

I was badly in need of another distraction, but I couldn't find anywhere to go but backwards—back to The Goddess, whose alleged silliness, and Melanie's cattiness in respect of it, had started the whole train off, whose helm was at least bejeweled and disguised.

"The Master must have spent a long time on The Goddess's jewelry," I observed. "That's an extensive set of designs—must have cost a fortune."

"It was a special commission," the receptionist said, her tone still radiating hostility to the model. "Hackwork, really—it wasn't the Master's own design, or at least not his original idea."

"Some rich man who wanted his favorite mistress to reflect his wealth, no doubt," I said. It was a joke, so I laughed. Melanie didn't.

"You shouldn't make salacious remarks while your girl-friend is suffering under the needle," the receptionist told me, although the scolding seemed a trifle off-hand, and I was sure that it wasn't the supposed betrayal of my own lady love that had occasioned her ill-humor.

"No, I shouldn't," I agreed. I looked at the bead curtain, which was trembling ever so slightly in resonance with the vibration of the tattooist's needle, but remained opaque. A faint voice—presumably Claire's—was audible, but there was no way to decipher what it was saying. I hoped that she hadn't strayed into confessional mode—not so much because I didn't want the tattooist to hear her confessions as because I didn't want to imagine that I might be missing them.

Thinking about Claire seemed, after all, to be the best distraction of all from the pain, and it didn't seem particularly improper, in the circumstances, to be thinking about her capacity to steer rather than Melanie's, or the fact that her nether region really did seem to have a French smoothness and silkiness rather than an Anglo-Saxon harshness, especially to a mind with an underlying neurological disposition that gave exceptional sensitivity to conscious caresses. Melanie could still see me, though, so I deliberately deflected my reminiscences to other parts of Claire's anatomy: to the smoothness of her breasts, the silkiness of her hair, the subtle movements of her hips and shoulder-blades, the precise texture of her abdomen. I had been conscious of it all, and intently so. I hadn't flinched once, or reflexively turned my face away from a single impending kiss.

Who wouldn't want to live forever, I thought, with such delights in the world?

Then I thought about the symbolism I'd read into the image of the bird and the flower as soon as I'd seen the Master's sketch, in which the flower was yet another symbolic vagina, surrendering its virginity with the customary sacrifice of blood—which Claire had not had to make, thanks to her habitual use of modern sanitary protection—although it was obviously not a magnolia, whose particular combination of white and pink recommended it for such recruitment in many works of French symbolism, but a rose. The word *rose* had more complex metaphorical implication, as evidenced by its immortalization by Edith Piaf, in her classic rendition of *La Vie en rose*....

The phone rang, and the receptionist answered it. It took a full three minutes for her to arrange and make a laborious left-handed note of an appointment for whoever was at the other end of the phone, during which I had no alternative but to remain silent and pensive, distracted from my deliberate self-distraction. I tried to begin thinking on a higher intellectual plane, about the hypothetical esthetics of the tattooist's art, but my mind seemed to be becoming duller by the minute, perhaps because the ibuprofen was kicking in. I couldn't seem to pick up any train of thought capable of running long distances.

"Have you worked here long?" I asked the receptionist, when the intellectual and conversational vacuum became oppressive.

"Since the shop opened," she said. "Even before that, I was his faithful Girl Friday. Every true artist needs someone to organize his work and his life—every male artist, at any rate. Males can't multitask, you see, and artists are away with the fairies half the time."

"I thought single-mindedness was supposed to a female attribute, according to you," I observed.

"Oh, it is. What takes hold of artists isn't single-mindedness—it's more like absent-mindedness, removal to another and more ethereal world. No male artist is really complete without someone to bear the burdens of the solid everyday world on his behalf."

I was tempted to say: "You're in love with him, then," but it seemed a step too far, especially since I'd already had two official warnings about chatting her up and sizing her up, so I didn't. I also rejected the possibility of making a joke about getting her own secret art at a discount, and the possibility of observing that she didn't look old enough to have been anyone's Girl Friday for very long. What I actually said was: "Do you have ambitions to become a tattooist yourself?"

She stared at me then, as if she weren't quite sure what I was implying. The expression suited her, but I kept a straight face, as if I were immune to her charms—as I was, given that I besotted with Claire. Eventually, she said: "Of course. I've used the needle often enough. The Master doesn't see my role as any kind of apprenticeship, but I do. For him, tattooing is much more than a mere trade, maybe even more than a fine art; he doesn't think of it as something teachable, so he doesn't try—but I'm learning anyway. When I use the needle, I'm doing trivial work, in his estimation, and maybe he's right to judge that I'm not doing the same thing as him, but that doesn't mean that I'm doing it wrong, or that what I'm doing isn't worthwhile."

"Will you set up in a studio of your own, eventually?" I queried.

"Probably. Time will tell."

"The unquiet spirit of Eddie Poe hasn't got into you yet," I joked. "It can only inhabit one person at a time, I guess, being unable to multitask."

Again, she didn't laugh. "He told you about that, did he?" she said. "What else did he say?"

"This and that," I said. "We were just exchanging light banter, playing with ideas. We talked about all sorts of things—nothing significant. I told him a story, but he didn't like it, and didn't reciprocate."

"What story?" she asked, curiously.

I repeated the story of the little girl and the secret of making nightingales sing by day, as I remembered it from the second-hand account someone had given to me. Melanie didn't like it either, and not because telling it in the shop might be bad for business. "That's revolting," she said. "Seriously nasty."

"That's the whole point," I countered. "It's a *conte cruel*." It seemed to be time to change the subject again. "I'm going to call my nightingale Luscinia," I remarked, idly.

She didn't take the revelation as lightly as I'd intended. "That's not a good idea," she said, soberly. "Titles are okay, because they're just for show, but names...did he tell you the real story?"

"What real story?" I asked.

"The real story of The Nightingale and the Rose. He should have told you...although it's just like him to hold it back, playing games with you. I won't try to tell it, I case I get it wrong, but you ought to read it. It's by Oscar Wilde."

"I know," I said. "That much he told me."

"Well, that's something. It would have been better if you hadn't known the other story. You have to be careful about associations of ideas—they can be dangerous. The nightingale is a part of you now, flesh of your flesh, and giving it a name will only exaggerate that shared identity. You *are* the work of art, remember—it's not just something drawn on your skin, which you can wash off."

"You told me not to wash it," I pointed out, "in case I damaged it."

"It can't be removed, though," she said. "People talk about having tattoos removed nowadays, but it's not as simple as it sounds. They can be concealed, but once they're a part of you, they're a part of you."

"Well," I said, less breezily than I might have hoped, "if that means that Claire and I will be together forever, bound into an atom of community by the work of art of which we're a part, I'll be very glad of it."

"How very romantic," the Goth girl remarked, with only a slight hint of corrosive cynicism. "I wish you the best of luck."

The phone rang again. This time, Melanie wasn't as polite as she had been to the first caller, and I saw her raise her eyes to the ceiling in mock-despair. "No," she said, "I'm afraid you can't speak to him. He's busy.... No, he'll be tied up for some time yet.... Yes, I will pass on the message.... Yes, I'm sure that he'll call you back.... Yes, I'll be sure to tell him that it's urgent.... I promise."

When she'd hung up the receiver she shook her head. "Bloody groupies!" she said. "It's bad enough when they come in reeking of steroids, itching to spread their legs, but when they start wanting to tell him all about their pornographic dreams.... I hope your girlfriend's not going to turn out to be one of *those*."

I resisted the temptation to tell her that the correct term for hypothetical hormones of sexual attraction was "pheromones", not "steroids". I was in the process of assuring her, a trifle stiffly, that I was sure that Claire wasn't the type to conceive an infatuation for her tattooist when someone came into the shop to make enquiries in person. Perhaps mercifully, it was a man, and Melanie didn't seem to mind his pheromones or testosterone at all. Our own conversation never got going again before she and I were both summoned back into the studio in order that Melanie could dress Claire's tattoo and run through the ritual instructions for a second time.

In the meantime, the Master tidied away his equipment, discarding all the needles into a special steel container.

We got back to my room in the Hall of Residence without any difficulty, but we soon found out that we were in no fit condition to make love that night, in any position whatsoever. After dinner, we talked long into the early hours, anticipating the time when the dressings could be cast aside and the peeling scabs would display our collaborative work of art in all its splendor. We were already looking forward to going back to the studio so that the artist could make a photographic record of his work—perhaps, if we were brave enough to grant permission, to be pinned up on his wall alongside the bejeweled lady and all the bats, snakes, dragons, hearts, spiders' webs and flowers.

Eventually, we did go to bed—together, because Claire didn't want to go back to her own room in a Hall on the other side of the campus—but we just lay side by side facing one another, me on my left side and her on her right, and tried to go to sleep. We must have succeeded in the end, because that was when the dreams started, at least for me: dreams in which Luscinia struggled in vain against her awful fate, singing plaintively all the while, and in which her lovely but bleak voice became my own pain, shrill and repetitive.

I prayed for daylight, but when it came within the dream—as it did inexorably—Luscinia kept on singing. Then, and only then, did I realize that her eyes were blind, scarred milk-white where some cruel hand had run red-hot needles into them...and I realized, belatedly, why Melanie the apprentice needlewoman had told me that it was a bad idea to give a name to the image in my tattoo, and to let the association of dangerous ideas have free play. A connection had been made that could not now be broken, or set aside.

Inevitably, Claire and I were somewhat distracted the following day by the publication of our exam results—we were both successful—and the expectation of graduation, but there was no way to avoid the rumor that ran round the campus like wildfire, even before the news was published in the local and national newspapers.

In broad daylight, shortly before three P.M., a tattooist named Devon Curtin had been murdered in his studio, in a shop named The Artificial Paradise, by means of a single gunshot to the head. The shooter had escaped unapprehended; the police were doing everything possible to identify him—or her.

CHAPTER FOUR

The police interviewed Claire and me separately, but the officers concerned were at pains to reassure us that we weren't suspects. They only wanted to know what Curtin had said to us while he was working on our tattoos. He had done others in the brief interim before he was killed, but they were all routine works of relatively short duration, which had involved little in the way of chitchat.

I told the police all that I could, none of which seemed relevant. It was slightly embarrassing listing the discourse on Paleolithic magic, the reference to the comic verse of Groucho Marx, the speculations about the inspirational ghost of Edgar Poe and the arguments as to whether the literal and the symbolic, or love and hate, were really opposites, but I tried not to leave anything out. The detectives didn't think any of it was relevant either, given that it was not the slightest use in identifying a possible suspect or motive, and they gave every appearance of being bored by my scrupulous completism.

I asked the policemen about Melanie, but they refused to comment; I discovered from the local TV news, however, that she was not a suspect, because the shooter had been seen on a closed-circuit TV that was monitoring the street, entering the shop immediately after Melanie had left it in order to carry the week's takings to the bank. The shooter had been unrecognizable, mainly because he—or she—was wearing a hooded jacket with the hood pulled up, but had clearly been a different individual. Closed-circuit TV footage was still a relative novelty then, so the fact that the perpetrator had been caught on video, however blurrily, almost seemed even more newsworthy than the murder itself.

That was the only genuinely interesting information that I was able to glean from the news coverage and my peripheral involvement in the affair. The fact that no one was ever charged with the crime never really registered on my consciousness, the awareness of the continued failure fading away gradually along with the news coverage itself. The tattoo provided a permanent reminder of the event, but even that became overlain by its effect as a reminder of other, more personal things. Within a matter of months, I no longer linked Luscinia automatically with Devon Curtin's murder, but with other more painful and more personal memories and issues.

For a start, Claire and I broke up. Our perfect love lasted less than a week, our relationship only a little longer.

In retrospect, that isn't particularly surprising. Everyone knows that sudden infatuations are prone to fade as quickly as they form, no matter how intense they are—especially infatuations conceived in unusual circumstances, such as the euphoria of eve-of-results parties, at which drugs are recklessly taken. On a common sense level, it would have been more surprising if our hectic fling had contrived to develop into something more durable. We were at the end of our university careers, about to go our separate ways; in order to remain together, or even to keep in touch, we would have had to throw out plans already conceived and make others, resisting pressures that were already being brought to bear.

We did try. We tried hard, in fact—but we didn't succeed. It's surprisingly easy to find things to argue about when you're trying to fuse together two lives with completely different histories and very different implicit trajectories. Coming together for sex is the simple part; the problems begin and cluster when you're out of bed, as soon as you begin to talk about matters more mundane than artistic tattoos.

In a matter of days, it seemed to me that Claire changed completely. After a further interval of time, of course, I recanted that suspicion, concluding that I had simply known nothing about her, in real terms, and had filled in all the gaps in my knowledge with a confabulation of optimistic hopes and desires. I had taken her for a delicate ingénue, as pure in mind and heart as her pale complexion, as meekly intricate in her personality as in her placid golden hair, and as soft in temperament as the marvelous texture of her beautiful skin. It took considerably less than seven days to realize that she wasn't really like that at all: that she was not only more robust in her ideas and opinions, but positively headstrong and stubborn. She had fixed views about the way things ought to be done, with which she wanted and expected me to conform—easy enough in bed, not so easy out of it. Nor did she have the hidden intellectual depths at which her initial quietness had hinted; her interests quickly came to seem much more commonplace, and—or so it seemed to me, given that I was something of an intellectual snob—considerably more vulgar. I expect that she had her own misapprehensions about me, for I failed equally conspicuously to live up to her expectations.

In brief, it had taken us a matter of hours to fall into love—or to jump, as it was something we were both seeking avidly rather than something that took us unawares—and it only took us a little longer to fall out again. The sum of our first bout of sex and our subsequent visit to The Artificial Paradise constituted the high point of our relationship; from that second sleepless night onwards, it was all downhill, gradually at first and then precipitately.

The relationship lingered on its deathbed for a little longer than it might have, because we were both reluctant to let it go, but the simple truth is that Devon Curtin's final masterpiece never was "seen" as it was supposed to be seen, even by a hypothetical observer who might have been standing by while we had sex, let alone by any actual observer or any kind of camera. As secret art went, it was certainly one of the best-kept secrets imaginable. By the time the scabs fell off, we were no longer making love, and we had no reason to pose as if we were, in order that a belated photographic record might be made of our brief folly.

The break-up was mutual; it wasn't inflicted by either one of us upon the other. I really don't know how Claire felt about it, during or afterwards, but I presume that she felt disappointment, frustration, resentment and all the other sour emotions that inevitably swarm around break-ups. I certainly did. In fact, I took it harder than I could ever have expected.

In those days, I had often tried to pose as a cynic with a heart of stone, and had had little difficulty falling for my own impostures, but I couldn't stand up to the acid test. When the pressure was exerted, I cracked. I didn't fall to pieces, but I definitely cracked. Luscinia's song became a record of my anguish, a plaintive echo of my confusion and misery. She sang by day and by night, always in desperation, as the fatal thorn plunged into her breast but somehow remained suspended, having only just penetrated its target. She bled and bled and bled, but she was an inexhaustible well, incapable of running dry.

I was transformed, and had no control over the manner of my transformation. I became a different person, astonished that I could still recognize myself.

Because no photographs were ever taken of The Nightingale and the Rose, no caption was ever attached to them, and no title was ever officially given to the work of art that we briefly sustained, and then tore in two—but no one could ever have been in doubt as to the fact that Devon Curtin would have called it The Nightingale and the Rose, or that its fragments ought to be called The Nightingale and The Rose. I alone had a different notion, a different title, and even I didn't call *myself* Luscinia. Luscinia was my *other* self, my *anima*, sometimes my heart and sometimes my soul, sometimes my anguish and sometimes my agony, but always my shadow, my ghost, my possessor, my reflection.

With Luscinia as part and parcel of my self, however, I quickly learned to see myself—perhaps far too readily—as a helpless creature, into whose heart a thorn was being plunged, and into whose blinded eyes red-hot needles had been inserted, who was slowly bleeding to death while held in a savage grip by a prickly briar.

I held Claire partly to blame for the disappointment and the distress, of course, but I knew even as I did so that she hadn't deceived me nearly as much as I had deceived myself, so I told myself repeatedly, if reluctantly, that I deserved my punishment, that I had made a fool of myself and invited disaster. The knowledge that the droplets of blood emerging from the nightingale's breast were supposed to be falling on to a white rose, staining it and transforming it, were easily added in to the metaphorical equation, and just as easily left out, as circumstances seemed to dictate. The whole affair seemed to have been a reckless spoliation, true love turned bloody, as scarlet as an open sore...but conclusively finished, conclusively sundered, with no possibility of any future reunion.

Life went on, however.

I had my degree; I had my career trajectory. I went to work for a translation agency, vaguely anticipating a steady flow of interesting literary works or at least a supply of upmarket porn. What I actually got was a steady trickle of ineffably tedious governmental reports, and a gradually rising flood of jargon-laden documents associated with the burgeoning Personal Computer industry. Because I was in on the latter almost at the beginning, I learned the jargon as it was invented, readily enough, and became efficient in its translation—an expertise that secured my steady employment, but trapped me in a professional location into which I had fallen more-or-less by accident, and which did not correspond at all with the visions and ambitions I had earlier entertained.

About a year after I saw Claire for the last time, I fell in love again—or jumped, as it was something I was extremely keen to do. Now that I had been introduced to the wonders of conscious touch, I was desperate to renew them, to find the true version of what had turned out to be false. It wasn't easy. I still had the same hang-ups that I'd endured throughout my adolescence, and however simple the remedy might be in theory, the process of working my way from casual acquaintance to lover, with all the contacts of eye and hand that implied, was an arduous business, requiring intense and unrelenting concentration. How I came to envy those whom my former psychotherapist would have called "neurotypical", to whom such contact came naturally, urged rather than inhibited by the autonomic nervous system! How I came to hate my own treacherous ANS, which offered me no answers at all, but only searching questions, all of whose key terms began with the syllable *conn*, the ultimate torture of Tantalus!

Perhaps I jumped too quickly. Perhaps I was so desperate to find a new love that I conjured it up where it did not really exist. Why even say *perhaps*? Is it not obvious? Well, perhaps. At the time, I thought it was real, just as I had thought my love for Claire was real. Perhaps it *was* real, and it was something else within me that was at fault, and not the love at all. I asked Luscinia, but she couldn't tell me. All she could do was sing the song of my doomed ambition.

The woman I married was Elizabeth Worrell, a teacher in a suburban secondary school in Maidenhead. She was taller than Claire—almost as tall as me—and more athletic. She was naturally pale, but she went to a tanning salon, in order that her bronzed skin might show off her golden hair to better advantage. The texture of her skin was a little firmer and a little rougher, perhaps partly in consequence of the tanning, but also because her subcutaneous musculature was more robust, possessed of greater strength. The same was true of her intimate regions, which did not yield as meekly as Claire's. At first, I thought her a poor substitute for a man of my delicate sensibilities, but the more we made love, the more her tone and texture became the norm, the standard according to which increasingly vague memories had to be measured and found wanting.

I learned a great deal more about the art and craft of love-making from Liz than I had ever learned from my brief affair with Claire. I was not her first; she had practiced skills. I benefited from the education, and developed skills of my own. The routines of our love-making helped me to relax somewhat, to suppress the rebellions of my ANS more easily—so long as we were actually engaged in the routines, in defined circumstances. Spontaneity was not my forte—which turned out to be a pity, because it was something Liz valued, and required. At first, the efforts involved in summoning up the consciousness and the concentration seemed well worthwhile, but as time went by, they became a source of private and secret resentment, because they went so largely unseen and unappreciated.

I did love Liz, however, sincerely and loyally. That love never faltered while we were together, but only became more steadfast. The feel of her body, and the mere fact of her presence, became extremely precious to me; my neurological disposition favored constancy as well as intensity; it appreciated marriage, and encouraged fidelity. As the early months of our marriage progressed, I loved her more and more: a mathematical progression, which more-or-less guaranteed that there would come a point when I loved her considerably more than she loved me. Her love was subject to no such acute consciousness, no such fervent concentration, no such irre-sistible increase.

We bought a small detached house in Maidenhead, set back from a residential street, squeezed into a triangular patch of land that had been isolated by the intersection of three angled rows of semi-detached houses. Its detachment, and the fact that it was almost in-visible from the road to which its house-number was affiliated, only accessible by a narrow and unobtrusive driveway, gave it a certain mystique and added commercial value, but detracted somewhat from any attempt to cultivate friendship with the neighbors. That did not matter, at least to me. My neurological disposition was extremely conducive to putting all my eggs in one basket.

After fourteen months of marriage, Liz gave birth to a daughter, whom we named Karen. That turned out to be the most significant event in my entire life.

Because I worked at home, on a flexible timetable that I could adapt to any and all contingencies, much of the burden of childcare fell upon me once Liz had returned to work full time. By that time, Karen could walk and talk, and was a real person rather than a mere bundle of needs and bodily functions. She was soft, and naturally affectionate. I never had the slightest negative reaction to her touch; my ANS was evidently capable of making exceptions. I was relaxed with Karen in a way that I'd never been relaxed before.

When Liz had returned to work, I took Karen to nursery in the mornings, picked her up at lunch-time, and looked after her until Liz got home. Later in the evenings, it was me who put Karen to bed and told her stories. Although I sometimes showed her the image of Luscinia, in response to her requests, I never told her the story that I had told Devon Curtin, which he and his receptionist had both deemed too horrid. When she asked about the thorn I told her the legend that Curtin had told me: that nightingales sang by night and pressed their breast against thorns because they had to stay awake, for fear of slow worms. That had its dark side too, although it wasn't as dark as "The Nightingale and the Rose", which I did eventually read to her, without having read it beforehand myself. It was, after all in a clearly-labeled book of "fairy tales", with no health warning whatsoever. Karen was about two months short of her fifth birthday at the time.

In Wilde's story, a young student is desperate to "dance" with a beautiful girl, who has promised that she will do so if he will bring her a red rose—but there are only white roses in his garden. A nightingale, hearing the student lament his fate, becomes convinced that his is the true love that she has long celebrated in her song, without ever finding much evidence of it in the world around her. She goes in search of a red rose, offering to sing her sweetest song in exchange, if any tree will provide her with one, but those trees whose roses are red have been spoiled by a late frost, and are incapable of producing flowers. One tree, however, tells the nightingale that a rose can be produced, if the nightingale will press her breast against a thorn and sing.

Convinced that Love is worth more than Life, the nightingale consents to the sacrifice. When she presses her breast against the thorn, a rose grows, pale and silvery at first, but gradually stained red by the nightingale's blood. The student finds the rose, and takes it to the girl, but she decides that it will not match her dress—and in any case, she has been sent a gift of diamonds by another suitor, which she prefers. The student throws the rose away in disgust, and decides that Love is silly, by comparison with Logic. He decides to devote himself to the study of philosophy instead.

When I read the story to Karen, she said: "That's horrid. Why did you read me such a horrid story?"

"It's a *conte cruel*," I told her. "It's deliberately subverting the expectation of a happy ending that's built into conventional fairy tales."

She wasn't yet five years old; if she understood what I was saying, she didn't care. "It's still horrid," she said—and I had to admit that she was right. I had to admit, having now read the Wilde story, that there wasn't that much to choose between that story and the one I'd told Devon Curtin, in terms of their essential horridness—which helped to explain, belatedly, why he had been a trifle reluctant to tell me exactly what he had in mind while I was in his studio, or even give me sufficient information to figure it out. It would probably have been different, though, if he'd ever got around to titling his piece, because the Wilde connection would then have been firmly made.

It was only a matter of weeks after I read "The Nightingale and the Rose" to Karen that Liz left me. The average time of her arrival home from work had been getting gradually later for some time, as Liz became increasingly involved in extracurricular activities. I use that term euphemistically; she wasn't coaching the netball team. When she eventually decided that she would rather live with her lover, whom she married shortly after the divorce, she took Karen with her. Losing Liz was bad enough, and would have counted as heartbreak on its own; losing Karen—of whom Liz inevitably got custody in the divorce settlement—more than doubled the anguish. To make matters worse, Liz and her lover found it politic to get jobs at a new school, in Bracknell, which was half an hour away by bus, with no direct train to make the journey faster. Because I worked at home, I had no car—I had never even learned to drive—so the bus was my only viable link with Karen, apart from the telephone. For the next ten years I spent a lot of hours on that Maidenhead-Bracknell bus, collecting Karen and taking her home again, and a lot more on the phone.

This time, I did fall to pieces, although I tried with all my might to hold the pieces together for Karen's sake. The terms of the custody agreement specified that Karen should visit me for weekends on a fortnightly basis, but Liz never raised any objection to our seeing one another more frequently than that, and Karen sometimes stayed with me for weeks at a time during school holidays. I never had to think about joining Fathers for Justice and masquerading as a superhero.

Distanced though it was by circumstance, my relationship with Karen remained close, at least in my estimation. It was the only substantial relationship I had that survived the divorce; most of the friends I'd had before had been Karen's friends more than mine. After a divorce, of course, one develops a sort of social leprosy; still-married people begin to feel uneasy in one's company, as if in fear of contagion.

The work kept flooding in, though, giving me every chance to immerse myself in it—an opportunity of which I took full advantage.

The aftermath of the divorce was when Luscinia really came into her own, perfecting her plaintive song. That was when she became St. Luscinia the Martyr, and the dreams reached their phantasmagoric extreme. In fact, they weren't really dreams because I wasn't really sleeping. I spent eight hours a night in bed, but I only dozed off for short intervals, strung out in series. Most of the time I just lay there, a victim of my thoughts, sensations and bitter regrets, which turned to deliria as my consciousness sank close to sleep without ever quite getting all the way there.

The identification became stronger than before, encouraged by the fact that Karen still asked, occasionally, to see the tattoo when I put her to bed and read her a story. Luscinia was in my flesh, part and parcel of my being, and perhaps the greater component of my soul. I *was* the martyred Nightingale, trapped and savaged by thorny circumstance, with a fibrous dagger impaling my heart—but I felt that I was no longer blind, that although I *had* been blind, especially in my love, I could now see.

That didn't stop me singing by day, but it turned my plaintive song into something far more sinister, deprived now of the slightest hint of loveliness, turned to pure torment. There were times when I longed to be unable to see: to have hot needles plunged into my eyes, if that were the price of restored innocence, of being able to reproduce the blithe song of careless nature—but there was not so much confusion between the literal and the symbolic as to make me conceive a plan to plunge actual needles into my eyes, or to give me the balls to do it even if I had ever formulated such a plan. In any case, I had to think about Karen. I had to hold my shattered self together for her sake.

Sometimes, I remembered the days when I had posed as a resilient cynic with a heart of stone, and wondered what had happened to that man, that bottle. Sometimes, I wondered whether the tattoo engraved on my side had been responsible for my transformation, instead of merely mirroring it. Sometimes, I wondered whether my separation from Claire, however inevitable, had left me crucially incomplete, unready and unable to cope with future vicissitudes of the heart. Sometimes, I wondered whether I might be laboring under a curse, imposed by means of Paleolithic magic in the cause of some unknown malevolence. Always, however, I came back to blaming myself, to cursing myself, to hating myself. I was the failure, the bird that had been unable to avoid the trap, unable to escape her dire fate, unable to conceive that her song might one day be perverted or stilled.

In time, the deliria faded into dreams, but the dreams were tenaciously recurrent. I sometimes woke up not knowing whether I was a man who had dreamed that he was a nightingale, or a nightingale who was now dreaming that she was a man. I honestly did not know which I ought to wish for, or which I would have chosen had any miracle ever given me the chance.

In my spare time—my dead, empty time—I usually watched television, precisely because it was mostly intellectually vacuous. I rarely read books any more for my own pleasure, my ambition to translate literary works having been cruelly betrayed, but I did read to Karen, and the habit continued long after she needed someone else to read to her. She liked the ritual element of it, and so did I. I avoided *contes cruels*, though, and never took the risk of investigating Hans Christian Andersen's tale about a nightingale.

That avoidance didn't stop me revisiting the symbolism of the tattoo repeatedly while St. Luscinia sang so persistently. When I had first seen Devon Curtin's sketch, I had assumed the symbolism of the piece to be quite straightforward: that it was a coded representation of the sexual act, the thorn entering the nightingale's breast symbolizing the penis, the drops of blood the semen, while the bird symbolized the outer parts of the vagina and the rose the inner parts, the threshold of the womb. Once I had read the Wilde story, however, I knew that Devon Curtin's reading of the symbolism of his art-work had to be markedly different.

It was easy enough, on occasion, to see myself as the self-sacrificing nightingale, who had surrendered her life's blood for the sake of an ideal of Love that eventuality had turned to dust. Had I, too, not given up on Love thereafter, in frank despair, in order to immerse myself in the logical and the abstract? This version seemed to fit my life-story even more comfortably than the tale I'd repeated. On other occasions, however, I realized that an interpretation of that sort was viewing the story in close up, and missing the bigger picture. If I was the nightingale in Devon Curtin's symbolic scheme, I thought, and Claire was the rose, then who was the student, and who was the girl? Were we both supposed to be playing dual roles? Was I both the student *and* the nightingale, in a combination as close and confused as that of bearer and tattoo? Was Claire both the rose *and* the girl who rejects it, as she had effectively torn apart the work of art in rejecting me? Had the tattooist, inspired by the spirit of Poe somehow understood, as soon as he saw us through his closed-circuit TV camera, that Claire and I were doomed to fall out of love as quickly as we had fallen into it, and had he conceived a complicated representation of our plight in a work of art that was doomed before it was begun? Or were there more pieces to the puzzle than I had ever previously suspected? Was the symbolic student the tattooist himself, forging both a nightingale and a rose for some further purpose, or for some further recipient, or for some further audience? Was there actually a girl at whom the whole project had somehow been aimed?

That last question, at least, provoked a possible answer. The Goddess, with her body decked out in all manner of illusory precious stones, seemed a plausible candidate. There must, after all, have been more to her relationship with the tattooist than that of canvas and artist, or his devoted Girl Friday would not have conceived such a fervent seemingly-jealous dislike for her.

I couldn't make a sensible story out of that hypothesis, though. I couldn't imagine any reason why Devon Curtin, even if he had been in love with the Goddess and the affair had gone awry, should have taken it into his head to produce The Nightingale and the Rose, for symbolic or magical purposes. He certainly hadn't given the impression of being in love with her when he had called her "Lydia"— although that, I knew, was the kind of psychological move that men sometimes made when they had been rejected by a woman. Might The Nightingale and the Rose have been a whimsical representation of his loss, or some kind of spell intended to lure her back? I couldn't see the logic of it, or the artistry.

Whatever the truth was, I had to suppose, the plan had been rendered redundant. It had never had a chance to come to fruition. Devon Curtin had been shot and killed before he could even take photographs of the dying nightingale and the transmogrifying rose, held in place by a simulation of the act of intercourse, let alone exhibit them—one way or another—to any other observer who might have perceived a personal meaning in the sequence of imagistic endeavors.

I remembered that the two policemen who had interviewed me about Devon Curtin's murder had not asked to see my tattoo, considering it utterly irrelevant to their enquiry, and I had not volunteered to show it to them, because I had made the same assumption. Now, I wondered. Now, I asked myself whether it was possible, however, remotely, that whatever relationship had prompted the tattooist to produce such a strange work of art, with the aid of two innocents who had walked in off the street, intoxicated by mutual infatuation, might indeed have had some connection with the motive for his murder.

It was, of course, far too late to go back to the police to make the suggestion, even though the case was still open. How, in any case, could I have explained the symbolism to them? Would I not have sounded like a lunatic? Did I not, in fact, sound like a lunatic? Was I not getting carried away by an old obsession, born of anguish and delirium?

Of course I sounded like a lunatic. Of course I was getting carried away by an obsession born of anguish and delirium. It didn't last forever, though. Anguish fades into dull despair; delirium gives way to authentic dream-sleep; in time, dreams fade too.

In time, St. Luscinia's song faded away. She never stopped dying, either by returning to health or completing the process, but she did stop ruffling her feathers, squirming in the grip of the briar, and—eventually—singing her terrible song.

Gradually, I began to bury the feelings and the memories. Gradually, I contrived to forget that I had a tattoo. If my eyes ever caught a glimpse of it, directly or in a mirror, my brain refused to register the fact. As the dreams and the song died away, so did the waking thoughts and ideas associated with them. As the waking thoughts and ideas became muted, the memories on which they were based became shielded and masked. Selective amnesia set in, without my being consciously aware of it—as is, I supposes, necessarily the case. I succeeded in avoided their touch, if not their reach.

Within three years of the divorce, matters didn't seem to be going from bad to worse any longer, although they didn't seem to be getting any better either. I remained a recluse, in my hidden house— I'd contrived to buy out Liz's equity in the financial settlement with the aid of a new mortgage—with Karen my only genuine visitor, although the postman called almost every day, even when most of my routine communication with the outer world had been transferred to email.

I did go out, and not just to catch the bus to Bracknell when it was time to collect Karen or take her back. I made a point of walking to the newsagents every morning rather than having a paper delivered, in order to ensure that I couldn't entirely escape exposure and regular exercise, and I went to the supermarket twice a week to maintain stocks of food and household essentials. Sometimes, I went to the central library to use the reference section. Sometimes, I just walked. I said "good morning" or "good afternoon" to any neighbors whose faces I recognized as I passed by, but I never said more and I always passed by. Karen often scolded me for it, and sometimes forced me out to eat in restaurants or go to the theater, but there was nothing she could do to control me when she wasn't there, as she usually wasn't during the week. By the time she was seventeen, on the threshold of adulthood, she had grown so used to what she called my "eccentricities" that she took them all for granted, and mostly reduced her disapproval to occasional despairing sighs. By then, I never read to her any more; even the ritual of it seemed to have become rather silly.

I might have gone on living like that—if you can call it living— indefinitely, perhaps until I died. But then J. K. Priestley, having plucked my name from a police evidence file and my address from the phone book, called on his way from his home in Twyford to his office in London, and it all came welling up again: the memories, the thoughts, the ideas, the dreams, the delusions and the questions.

The empire of logic tottered, and Luscinia resumed her song.

PART TWO

SEEKING CONNAISSANCE

CHAPTER FIVE

Again, it was about ten-thirty in the morning, on the day after J. K. Priestley's visit, that the doorbell rang again. I was in the study again, trying to work, but that wasn't why the interruption annoyed me. The coincidence of timing caused me to jump to the conclusion that Priestley had returned, eager to take a second shot at persuading me to appear in his exhibition, one way or another.

I'd looked up Devon Curtin upon the internet the night before. It had been late, and I hadn't lingered long over the search and its corollary links, but I'd seen more than enough to open my eyes. The first hits that came up were all news items and publicity material about the upcoming exhibition, which waxed lyrical about the current fad that had elevated tattooing to the status of a fashionable art, and Devon Curtin to cult status. The fact that his alleged genius had been nipped in the bud, cut short by a murder that had never been solved, had obviously added greatly to his chances of acquiring cult status, by surrounding him with implications of lost potential and a shroud of mystery.

There were several sites displaying his flash designs and photographs of his artier works. Unsurprisingly, the ones he'd displayed in his front office and workshop still figured as his most celebrated: The Falling Angel, The Tree of the Knowledge of Good and Evil, The Book of Shadows, The Masque of the Red Death, The Golden Dragon and, of course, The Goddess.

The Goddess, it seemed, had become something of a mystery. Her name was known, but not her whereabouts. Apparently, she had left the country not long after the murder, and no one knew where she had gone. No one had tried to stop her because she was not regarded as a suspect in Curtin's murder, apparently having been in possession of a good alibi. No one knew why she had left either, so far as I can tell, although the fact that a number of sites took the trouble to point that out gave the datum a slightly sinister nuance. She was, however, abundantly featured in photographic form—more, I assumed, because she was stark naked than because of the esthetic merits of her embellishments.

It was on the sites that remarked on the mystery of the Goddess's disappearance that I first saw references to The Nightingale and The Rose—in that precise manner, as separate entities. They completed the trinity of Curtin's "missing works", although I assumed that there must be numerous others that had gone unremarked and had thus avoided particular attention. Because our names were unknown—no one else, apparently, had obtained access to Melanie's notebook until the exhibition organizers had persuaded the police to let them do so—and because there were no photographs of the tattoos on file, even the very existence of the two tattoos had a quasi-legendary aura about it. Presumably, its existence was only known because Melanie had spread the news around of what had taken place in the studio on the eve of the murder.

At any rate, it seemed—even on the basis of a cursory flick through the hits, which lasted no more than a few minutes—that I had unknowingly acquired a certain perverse celebrity, not under my name but under half a title. I cursed that discovery, figuring that J. K. Priestley might not be the only person eager to meet me, or at least get a look at me in the flesh, even fully clothed. What, I wondered, would Karen make of it if and when she found out? What would Claire make of it, if she wasn't already aware of her own perversely pseudonymous fame?

I saw enough even on the news sites to figure out that the upcoming exhibition might be crucial, not merely to Devon Curtin's posthumous career and reputation, but to the entire crusade that had been undertaken on behalf of tattooing as a Fine Art. If the event drew a large enough audience, it would not only establish Curtin's cult status, providing the cause with an essential martyr, but would clear the way for living artists in the same line of work to enjoy a considerable boost in their fortunes. Tattooing for art's sake was still, and would probably always remain, somewhat esoteric—but minorities vary greatly in size and wealth, and I could understand the logic of the fact that fads in the world of high fashion could stimulate the flow of millions, if not billions, of pounds.

When I switched off the computer I resolved to resume the search the following day, in order to push the investigation further into the remoter hits, in the hope of finding out a little more about my strange and shadowy reputation, and about the inspiration behind Devon Curtin's work. Now that he had become a cult figure, I reckoned, there were bound to be essays by fans and scholars regarding the symbolism of his work, which might help to cast some light on the motive behind The Nightingale and the Rose and its relation, if any, to The Goddess. When I got up the next morning, however, I thought that I ought at least to try to do some work first, in order not to fall too far behind my schedule. I tended to be a trifle obsessive about my schedule, and to get anxious when it was disrupted—I had learned from the web that that was another of what the university shrink would have called "Asperger's traits".

Even so, I would have been glad to break off from a task that had come to seem even more tedious than usual if it hadn't been for the sinking feeling in my abdomen derived from the suspicion that J. K. the Connoisseur was calling in on his way to work again, having armed himself for a new assault.

I opened the door ready and willing to be rude, but the wind was taken right out of my sails when I saw that the car standing in the driveway was a red Citroen rather than a grey Volvo, and that the person standing in the porch wasn't J. K. Priestley at all but a woman in her early forties. She was wearing a tan raincoat and carrying a collapsible umbrella as well as a voluminous black handbag. The early morning drizzle had stopped, but the sky was still ominously grey.

"Hello Cris," she said. "May I come in?"

She had been poised too as the door opened, and had had no intention of waiting for an answer to her question. She swept past me with total confidence that I would stand aside. Automatically, I did—my helplessness increased by the fact that I didn't recognize her, and couldn't figure out, for the moment, how she knew my name.

She paused in the hallway and waited for me to point her in the direction of the sitting room. She strode in and paused again, surveying the room with a long panning glance, which took in the bookshelves, the faded prints of Mucha posters on the wall, the framed photos of Karen on the mantelpiece, the non-plasma television, the obsolete video equipment, the worn sofa and the less-worn matching armchairs, the uncleared coffee-table and the wheeled radiator, whose indicator light was glowing red although the room didn't seem warm. I never turned the heat up in the sitting room until I finished work in the study.

"Do you ever clean this place?" she asked. I was astonished that she should take such a liberty; casual insults of that sort had long been the sole prerogative of my ex-wife.

"Whenever I have visitors," I said. "Expected visitors, that is." I didn't feel that it was necessary to explain that I only ever had one visitor; I did, after all, clean the bathroom and vacuum the carpets before her every expected visit.

My unexpected visitor turned around then. "You don't recognize me, do you?" she said.

"No," I said. She had brown hair and brown eyes; her face gave the impression that it had once been thinner, and had only recently begun to fill out. The bulky raincoat concealed her figure, but there was enough breadth there to give a similar impression. She was still attractive, by the standards of women past forty, but there was a distinct suggestion of faded glory about her. That obviously hadn't dented her self-confidence at all, because her gaze was imperious; she believed that her charms still had the power to command men's attention and humility, and the belief would probably be self-justifying for a while longer.

"I'm Melanie Millward," she said. "We only met once, but I remember you. The circumstances made it difficult to forget. Not that I'd have recognized you if I'd passed you in the street, mind—you've changed a lot."

By the time she got to the end of the final sentence I had caught on. "I wouldn't have recognized you either," I said, "even if your shoulders were bare. Maybe if your hair were still dyed black and you were wearing a leopard-skin-patterned ersatz silk top." The wind of hostility was picking up my sails again as I realized that she must be here for exactly the same reason as Priestley, quite possibly at his request. Having failed himself, he had sent in a seductress—of sorts.

"At least you remember me," she said. "That spares me some embarrassment. It would be terrible if you didn't remember trying to chat me up while you were recuperating from your ordeal."

A denial was on the tip of my tongue, but I realized in time that she was trying to wind me up. Instead, I put on the most ostentatiously fake tone of politeness I could contrive, and said: "What can I do for you, Ms. Millward?" I was trying not to think of any words beginning with *conn*, but I knew that it wasn't going to be easy. Suddenly, she seemed to be considerably more attractive, or at least a good deal sexier. I *did* remember her.

She obviously wanted to tease me a little more before she spelled out what it was that I could do for her, so she took off her raincoat, with just a hint of rhythmic smoothness and exaggerated slowness about her movements. If she was trying to do an impression of a stripper beginning a routine it was largely wasted on me; I had never seen a strip-tease in the flesh—but I was in little doubt as to her capacity to steer me in whatever direction she pleased, if she really put her mind to it.

She handed me the coat and I took it.

"Would you like a cup of tea?" I asked, in the same insincerely polite tone.

"Please," she said. "Milk, no sugar." Then she turned her back on me again, in the obvious expectation that I was about to leave the room.

I left. I hung her coat on a peg in the hallway and went into the kitchen to switch the kettle on. I stayed to watch it boil after I'd put the tea bags in the mugs, taking the opportunity to think.

I wasn't at all nervous. I held all the cards. I had every intention of sticking to my stubborn refusal, and I firmly believed that there wasn't a thing that Devon Curtin's former receptionist could do about it. Presumably she had become the custodian of his memory, perhaps also of his photographs; she might well have a great deal riding on the success of the planned exhibition—but so what? I didn't owe her anything. Luscinia was mine, and mine alone. I had the sovereign rights of a work of art, including the right to remain silent and secret.

I was aware of the nightingale's presence under my arm, where she seemed to be in hiding, determined once again to sing, but for my inner ears only. She didn't have any ambition to show herself, to *be seen*.

When I brought the mugs of tea into the sitting room Melanie Millward was standing by the fireplace, holding one of the framed photographs from the mantelpiece in her left hand.

"Is this your family?" she asked, innocently, before putting it back, taking the tea, and sitting down on the sofa—which, as she must have realized, was where I usually sat.

"That's an old photograph," I admitted, tersely, as I perched on one of the armchairs. "Karen's seventeen now—she's only three there. The other photographs are all of her at various ages." I didn't mention Liz at all; her absence from the house, and my life, was presumably as obvious as her belated presence in the picture.

"I never married," she said. "Just like Devon: always faithful to my art, never to my clients—not in that way, at least. Did you know that I took over The Artificial Paradise? I ran the shop for thirteen years after Devon's death, with the help of a couple of assistants. You never came back in—I'd have recognized you if you had. I saw your girl-friend a couple of times, but not in the shop. The police talked to you both, didn't they?"

"They interviewed us about what Curtin said to us while he was working on us. We weren't able to tell them anything useful. They must have interviewed you far more intensively—you were in a far better position than we were to offer suggestions about motives and suspects."

"Not really," she said. "I had no more idea who might have shot him, or why, than you did. You know that it wasn't me, right?"

"I did hear something about an alibi provided by closed-circuit TV in the street."

"Right. They showed me the video, in the hope that I might recognize him, but I couldn't, He was a real trend-setter, though, sporting a hoodie some time before it became standard business-wear for all petty criminals."

"It was a *he*, then?" I said.

"Presumably. The pictures weren't clear enough for the police to be absolutely sure. They seemed to think that the murder might have something to do with drugs, but Devon's coke habit was under control, and I'm certain that he wasn't in debt to any dealers. I was only allowed to keep his appointment-book, because he didn't think my arithmetic was up to doing the accounts, but I'm sure there was nothing dodgy about the shop's finances—although that didn't stop the cops from keeping the ledger as evidence, along with the appointment-book and everything else. Bloody nuisance, that."

"What do you think it was to do with, then?" I demanded. I was sitting bolt upright, with my tea-cup held defensively in front of me, but it wasn't big enough to intercept her gaze as she scanned my torso time and time again, as if sheer persistence might somehow allow her to penetrate the shirt and pullover. She, of course, had seen Luscinia before—but only as an inflamed wound, her image obscured by side-effects of the stinging needle.

"I just told you that I had no idea," she said, with a hint of a snarl. "I had no idea then, and I still don't."

"You didn't think it might have something to do with The Goddess?" I prompted.

She seemed genuinely surprised—which surprised me slightly, given that J. K. Priestley had been so quick to deny that it had, even without an explicit prompt. "No," she said. "Nobody would shoot anyone over that stupid…woman." She had obviously learned to restrain her language in polite company—not that either of us was trying overly hard to be polite.

"But you're certain it wasn't Armina Holliman who fired the shot? It was presumably you who told J. K. Priestley that it definitely wasn't her."

Again, she was taken by surprise. "Jakey didn't mention that he'd talked to you about Armina Holliman," she said. "He couldn't possibly have entertained any serious hope that you might know where she is."

"He did send you here, then? He thinks you have a better chance of persuading me to play ball than he had. Well, he's wrong. I said no and I mean no. I'm sorry, if you have high hopes invested in the exhibition, but that's the way it is. I've no intention of making an exhibition of myself."

Melanie Millward leaned forward in order to put her tea down on the coffee-table, between the previous evening's coffee-mug and a plate scattered with stale cake-crumbs. Then she squared up, as if making ready for combat. "First of all," she said. "Jakey didn't *send* me. He's working for me, not the other way around—although he might not think of it that way, since he has a personal interest as well as a commercial interest in the affair. Secondly, I didn't come to *persuade* you. I can't imagine for the life of me why you would need persuading—why you aren't eager to jump at the chance I'm offering. You don't have anything to lose, and if appearances can be trusted, you might have everything to gain—a life, for example. You're a work of art, and you're surely not stupid enough to pretend that you don't know that, or that you don't like it. What the hell is your purpose here on Earth if not to make an exhibition of yourself, given the opportunity? Well, I'm giving you the opportunity. You'd be insane not to take it. I came to point that out—and, if necessary, to shake some sense into you."

It wasn't the assault I'd been expecting, and it did put me on the wrong foot, making the arguments I'd prepared seem quite redundant. With no defense ready, I was reduced to procrastination. "I'm only the half the picture," I said, lamely, "and wasn't it you who gave me a lecture on tattooing being the secret art?"

"Are you saying that you don't want to see your lovely little Claire again, under any circumstances?" she countered. "Is that why you were so adamant in your refusal? It was twenty years ago, for God's sake. How bad can a break-up still seem, after all that time? You were sufficiently convinced that you were in love when you came into the shop to hand over your credit card immediately when Devon offered to make the pair of you two halves of the same work of art—how can you be less than intrigued by the possibility of putting it together again? I can see that her husband might not like the idea, if she turns out to be married, but what reason could *you* possibly have for not wanting to see her again, even if she did break your heart? It's not as if it hasn't been broken since, is it?"

I didn't know how much she'd been able to find out about me since the reluctant evidence file had disclosed my name, but even if the catty remark was guesswork based on a glance around the room, I knew how telling that glance must have been, and how reliable. I knew that I must be an open book myself, easily readable even to those without an artist's discriminating eye. I was prepared to assume that she did have an artist's discriminating eye, if not a bookkeeper's talent for arithmetic, and that she hadn't run Devon Curtin's tattoo parlor for thirteen years merely as a petty businesswoman. I hadn't continued my internet search far enough to gather any abundant detail about Curtin's legacy, but I was prepared to assume that Melanie Millward had made every effort to continue his work as well as popularizing it, playing Plato to his Socrates…or, at least, Baudelaire to his Poe.

I took a long swig of tea, to cover my continuing unreadiness to get stuck into the argument. "It has nothing to do with Claire," I said, finally. "It's just me. I simply don't want to do it. Maybe I do have custody of something that's now thought to be a significant work of art, but that doesn't mean that I have an obligation to show it."

"Actually," she said, "it does." Her voice was less insistent, though, and more contemplative. Having apparently mistaken the reason for my reluctance, she was now casting about for another hypothesis. Her eyes were studying me, but she no longer seemed fierce—certainly not as fierce as she had seemed twenty years before, clad as a panther.

"We'll have to disagree about that," I said. "It's my tattoo, and I can keep it covered up if I want to. End of story."

"The question is," she countered, "why do you want to?"

"I don't have to answer your questions, either."

After a slight pause, she said: "I guess not—but I wish you would. Don't you think, in the circumstances, that the least you owe me is an explanation?"

That was a difficult one, because I could see why she might think that I did. That was the nub of the matter, though. The real basis of my reluctance—of my determination—was that I didn't believe that I could explain Luscinia to anyone, and certainly didn't want to try, not for fear of convincing them that I was insane, but for fear of convincing myself that I was insane. While the haunting remained secret, it was a question I didn't have to ask, let alone answer, but if it were ever exposed....

"I just don't want to do it," I insisted. "I don't need your money, so I can't be bribed—or seduced."

I shouldn't have supplied the addendum; it gave her a point of leverage. "I gave that possibility serious consideration on the way over," she said, a trifle contemptuously. "If the only way I could get to see the tattoo was to get you into bed, I figured, it was a price worth paying—but I was thinking of you then as you were twenty years ago. You were beautiful then, and full of life. Now, not so much."

"You don't look so great yourself at forty-something, without all the Gothic gear," I retorted.

She smiled. "*Touché*. Time takes its toll on us all, and we all hear the knell of doom in the end. I'm not going to get into a big argument about my fading looks, though. If you won't give me a chance to counter your reasons for refusing to lend yourself to the exhibition, I'll just move on to plan B. All this is a little premature anyway, given that we haven't located Claire yet. Just hypothetically, suppose that we do—and that she's willing, even enthusiastic, to do it? Suppose *she* were to come round to...persuade you. What then?"

What indeed? But there was an obvious countermove to that gambit. "Just hypothetically, suppose that if and when you find her, she reacts exactly as I did. What then?"

Melanie Millward pursed her lips slightly, but she wasn't about to be put off so easily. "Can you understand how serious a matter your absence from the exhibition would be?" she said. "We have plenty of items in hand, even if we don't find Armina—who might well be impossible to locate, given that she fled the country twenty years ago and doesn't seem to have been back since—but The

Nightingale and The Rose are special. For one thing, it's the only duet he ever did; for another, we don't even have a photographic record of it. Add to that the fact that it was his last major piece, his swan song, and you can surely comprehend its significance within his canon. I don't deny that there's money at stake here, but that's not my principal motivation. Devon's future reputation depends on this exhibition; it's the definitive testament to his endeavor as an artist; it's the measure of his achievement. If we don't have *you*, at least as a photographic image—even without Claire, in the unlikely event that we can't find her—that measure will fall short.

"I need you, Cris—but more importantly, Devon needs you. He may be dead, but an artist's needs survive him, growing rather than diminishing with his demise. You don't owe me anything, but you do owe *him* something, and it would be a serious act of betrayal to deny him. If you won't lend us your flesh, then at least let us provide an adequate photographic record. At the very least, take some photographs yourself, on a mobile phone if you can't stand the thought of exposing yourself to a video camera. Needless to say, we'll lend you any equipment you'll consent to use. If you can bring yourself to pose the entire work, that would obviously be an order of magnitude better than just raising your own arm and standing alone, but anything would be better than nothing. Please give us something, Cris—for Devon's sake. You rather liked him, as I recall. You talked to him about all the usual rubbish—Paleolithic magic, the confusion of opposites, the spirit of Eddie Poe—and seem to have got along like a house on fire. Didn't you even tell him a story about the secret of making nightingales sing by day?"

She broke off, her gaze narrowing. I wasn't aware of having reacted in any way, but something must have shown in my face. "Did you ever read the Wilde story?" she asked, suddenly.

"Yes. I read it aloud to my daughter. I probably wouldn't have, if I'd known how it ended, but it was in a book of fairy tales. How was I to know that it was a *conte cruel*?"

"The secret art," she echoed, reflectively. "You weren't talking about clothing, were you? You really are nurturing some kind of secret—something that makes you intent on keeping the tattoo unexposed. Do you have *bad dreams*, Cris?"

"Why?" I said. "Do you?" She didn't flinch, but I got the impression that she had to tense herself in order to avoid it. I guessed immediately that she and I weren't the only ones—but you can't mount an exhibition of dreams, even with the help of a top-flight professional curator with experience at the V&A.

"It's not magic," I hastened to add. "It's perfectly natural. People get tattoos in order to express themselves, choosing imagery that reflects some aspect of their personality, more likely than not the same aspect of their personality that's most readily reflected in their dreams. Once they have it, it becomes even more likely to be reflected in their dreams. I didn't choose mine, but that doesn't alter the situation. Once I had her engraved in my flesh, how could I help identifying with her, recruiting her into the play and substance of the conscious and unconscious parts of my mind?"

"Her?"

"Wilde's nightingale is female."

"But you didn't know that until you read the story aloud to your daughter—you just said that you didn't know how it ended." She paused, and then said: "Luscinia. You actually told me that you were going to call your nightingale that, didn't you? I remember now."

I was surprised that she had remembered, but too determined to keep control of myself to express the surprise openly, or anything else. Nor was I about to point out that the distinction between the literal and the symbolic might not be as clear as was sometimes imagined. I had no more tea to sip, though, so I simply stayed silent.

"You're making a mistake," she opined, eventually.

"How so?"

"I don't know what sort of nightmares you've had, or how the image in the tattoo figured in them—although, as you've obviously deduced, other recipients of Devon's art-work have experienced something similar, and you're quite right to say that there's nothing supernatural about it, and that it's entirely understandable in psychological terms—but it's a mistake to hoard the nightmares away, trying to lock them up and imprison them. It really would be better for you to expose them to the light of day, photographically if not in the flesh. Refusing to take part in the exhibition is a mistake, as well as a betrayal."

"I don't agree that it's either."

She stood up abruptly. "I'd like to see the tattoo, please," she said, bluntly.

"You want me to take off my pullover and my shirt? Here and now?"

"Yes."

"No."

"What are you afraid of? Do you want to see mine?" As she spoke she took off her jacket. She was wearing a sleeveless top underneath, so the gesture exposed the tattoos on her upper arms. I'd only remembered them vaguely, but as soon as I saw them, I recognized them. Then she pulled down the shoulder-straps of the top, and pushed it down to her waist. She reached around her back, aiming for the clasp of her bra. I didn't have the slightest doubt that she would take it off, and continue by pulling down her skirt, taking off her tights, and perhaps her knickers as well. Suddenly, I was anxious, almost paralyzed.

"Stop!" I said.

She stopped—but her expression was a naked challenge, an evident threat. The offer was clear; she would stop or continue, as I wished, but she would only do what I asked if I offered a *quid pro quo*.

There were tattoos all over her torso, extending the pattern of those on her shoulders—especially the curlicues. The ensemble wasn't an item of representative art, like The Golden Dragon or The Tree of the Knowledge of Good and Evil; it was far more abstract than that. Some of the shapes were bats or hieroglyphs, but many were little more than mere swirls; they didn't seem to be transforming her into something else, but merely emphasizing the contours of her own body, her own self.

I assumed that the entire design required her to stand naked, or almost naked, in order to be savored in its fullness, its lushness, its completeness. She was obviously accustomed to making an exhibition of herself, and would not have hesitated to perform a duet rather than a solo, if she had had the opportunity and the requirement.

Slowly, I took off my pullover. Then I unbuttoned my shirt, and opened it up, as I had done so many times for Karen when she was smaller. Then I lifted my arm to expose Luscinia, helpless in the embrace of her thorny assassin.

Melanie Millward didn't over-exaggerate her inspection, nor did she whip out a digital camera and demand to take a photograph. Apparently, she was prepared to proceed one step at a time. She just looked, and then nodded in satisfaction.

"Thanks, Cris" she said.

While I re-adjusted my clothing, she re-adjusted hers. I knew—and knew that she knew—that things had changed, that the balance of authority had been firmly established, and that she was in control. That didn't mean, however, that I was making any promises, or accepting any obligations. I wanted more time to think, more time to rationalize my position.

She seemed to understand that. She sat down on the sofa again, and I resumed my position in the armchair. It was just a truce, though.

Feeling that she now owed me one, and wanting to take advantage of the implicit intimacy we'd just shared, I said: "Were you Devon Curtin's lover as well as his apprentice."

"That's a rather coy way of putting it," she said. "We fucked. We weren't *in love*, like you and little Claire. It was no big deal." The last statement, at least rang hollow. I estimated that it was probably half true—that it had been no big deal for him, but not necessarily for her.

"What about the Goddess?"

"Why are you so interested in *her*?"

"I remember that you were nasty about her while I was recuperating from the ordeal," I said—but then I repented my dishonesty. "Actually," I added, "I've been wondering every since I read the Wilde story whether there was some connection between my tattoo and hers—whether, in Devon Curtin's mind, she might be the girl in the story who preferred the diamonds to the red rose?"

"I haven't a clue," she retorted, apparently quite frankly. "Devon never said anything to me about The Goddess being relevant, although he did tell me the story of the Nightingale and the Rose—I recognized it the moment he showed you the sketch, and knew it was a piece he'd wanted to do for some time. He was a big fan of Wilde, as well as Poe. The Goddess wasn't even his idea—someone else paid him to do it, and provided the design—and before you ask, I don't know who it was. The transaction went through the accounts in the normal way, but the only name recorded in the appointment-book was Armina Holliman's. It can't have been her husband; she was divorced. I suppose it might have been what you'd call her lover, if she had one." Again, the final sentence lacked all conviction.

If Melanie had been jealous when Devon screwed Armina, I thought, perhaps she hadn't been the only one. Perhaps the shooting had been a crime of passion. I didn't voice the hypothesis, though—it seemed a trifle clichéd.

"You're hooked, aren't you?" the ex-receptionist said, then. "You might still be shy about showing off the tattoo, but you're as hooked as anyone else on the artistry and mystery of Devon's work? How could you avoid it, given that you're a key example of both? It really is a good piece of work, you know—not very large, to be sure, but beautifully detailed. I'd love to see the whole thing, properly posed…and properly animated. Pity that'll never happen again—by which I mean that no one will ever see you and Claire making love as you once were: twenty years old and beautiful. It wouldn't be the same watching a wreck like you toiling over some forty-year-old mother, no matter how good the ink-work is."

I knew that she was being deliberately provocative, still trying to wind me up, but I winced anyway.

"The moment has gone," she continued, ruthlessly. "All that's left is an echo. On the other hand, if you and Claire *were* willing to video yourselves in action, tats to the camera, even now, at forty….you could probably make a tidy sum selling copies to aficionados. Have you checked out the lunatic fringe on the internet? You have to scroll down a fair way, unless you use the right keywords, but you can get there by coupling Devon's name with 'magic' or 'curse'. Try it and see."

"So you think that Curtin really was trying to work magic with his tattoos?" I said.

"No, damn it! That was just a line of patter—he was a cokehead, not a nutter. That didn't prevent some of his crazy clients projecting their craziness on to him. Some of them certainly believed that he had powers."

"Including the Goddess?"

The ex-receptionist rolled her eyes, protesting against the apparent obsession. "I don't know—I'll ask her if and when we find her. Quite probably—she was daft enough. Does it matter?" She stood up and looked me in the eye.

I avoided her gaze and went to fetch her coat. Like J. K. Priestley, she certainly hadn't given up; she was just mounting a tactical retreat, knowing that she had three months to change my mind. She was obviously prepared for a war of attrition.

"You have Jakey's card," she said, as I helped her into her coat. "Keep it safe. When you've had time to think, I suspect you'll come round to our way of thinking. I'll be in touch again, as soon as we've located your lost love—and don't try to tell me that you won't thank us for it, because I wouldn't believe you. You should be grateful for the excuse, not only to get together with her again, but to screw her for art's sake. How many men get that sort of edge in the great game?"

I made no response as I showed her to the door. It had begun raining again, and she unfolded her umbrella in the porch to protect her while she walked to her car.

"I really do think you'd find it a valuable experience to help us out," she said, in a softer tone of voice that didn't really suit her. Her eyes strayed over the weeds on the driveway to the anonymous lumps of greenery that had once been rhododendron bushes, but she didn't make any further remark about the state of my existence or the extent to which I'd let things slide. "Think it over."

She ambled away toward the red Citroen—but I knew that she'd be back, probably with reinforcements. To make things worse, I knew that there was some truth in what she said. If and when they found Claire, and insisted on bring us together, I would be grateful—and there was no way in the world, now, that I could avoid thinking it over...and over and over and over.

CHAPTER SIX

At lunch-time, I called Karen, even though I wasn't supposed to call her on her mobile, and certainly not while she was at school. "Can you come over this evening, Beauty?" I asked. "There's something I need to ask your advice about."

"I've got plans," she said, "and you know that Mum doesn't really like me coming to see you during the week. This term is the last real teaching we get before the exams—after Easter it's all study leave. Ask me now."

"I've been asked to be in an exhibition," I said, after only a moment's hesitation. "Displaying my tattoo."

"You mean standing there naked to the waist?" she said, incredulously, after a moment's pause for thought.

"Standing," I said, echoing J. K. Priestley, "isn't what they have in mind."

I was expecting her to be horrified. I was expecting her to forbid it. I was expecting her to provide me with an excuse, a weapon to use in the impending war against Melanie Millward. I was disappointed.

"Cool," she said. "Have they found your old girl-friend for you? How long will you have to lie on top of her—at a stretch, I mean?" She giggled at the slight joke.

"All your friends would see me," I said, exaggerating in the cause of desperation.

"I'll make sure they do," she assured me. "I'll ask my form teacher if she can organize a school trip, as long as it doesn't clash with the exams."

I couldn't confess to her that I'd hoped for a very different response. I hadn't a clue whether she knew that and was just teasing me, or whether she meant every word.

"I'll ring you back," she said. "I'll try to come over at the weekend—probably Sunday."

"Thanks," I said, although it was only Thursday. Then the doorbell rang yet again. I thought at first that Melanie Millward must have forgotten something, and looked around to see what it might be. She hadn't.

I went to the door and opened it cautiously.

The man standing on the doorstep wasn't J. K. Priestley, although he was about the same age and height. He wasn't nearly as well-dressed, and he looked more like a laborer than a solicitor. I didn't recognize him, but, circumstances being what they were, I searched my memories of twenty years before, just in case his younger self was lurking somewhere within them. Then I looked at the white van parked in the drive, and read the legend inscribed, in a somewhat amateurish manner, on the side: STANLEY MORE, GARDENING SERVICES.

I could understand why a gardener touting for business might think of my overgrown and tangled private wilderness as a Garden of Eden ready to pour out a stream of financial benefits, but I couldn't understand how he'd seen it from the road if he was just passing by. I was gathering myself to tell him that I really didn't care enough to part with the kind of money he'd doubtless demand in exchange for clearing it up when he got in first.

"I'm sorry to bother you, sir," he said, "but I wonder if you might once have been acquainted with a man named Devon Curtin?"

The surprise was, of course, dulled by the expectation I'd already formed that more people were going to beat a path to my door in search of that particular mousetrap, but Stanley More didn't seem to fit the part.

"I don't give out information on the doorstep," I told him, weakly.

"That's understandable, sir," he said. "I knew him myself, you see. I was one of his clients. I've been asked to appear in an exhibition of his work."

"Did Melanie Millward send you?" I asked, more puzzled than annoyed.

"Not exactly, sir," he said. "I did follow her here, though. I was curious."

I had dire suspicions as to why he was curious, and what about, and I wasn't about to let him into the house. I moved backward reflexively, and half-closed the door so that it would serve as a symbolic defense. "I told her that I didn't want to appear in her exhibition," I said, not knowing what else to say. "She didn't seem to want to take no for an answer, but that's her problem, not mine."

"I said yes," the mysterious stranger informed me. "I could do with the money, but that's not the issue. Kim—that's The Falling Angel—is on board too, and Howard the Serpent Prince, but The Masque doesn't get out much any more, and isn't really in a fit condition to exhibit himself. Some of us used to meet up back in the day, you know…to talk things over. I'm The Tree of the Knowledge of Good and Evil, by the way—perhaps you've seen me before, at least from the back?"

I wasn't sure whether I ought to admit it or not, but in the end I nodded. "I remember the tree tattoo, vaguely," I admitted.

He nodded, in apparent satisfaction. "I ought to say, Mr. Ellsworth," he pronounced, sententiously, "that it's a privilege to be standing in the presence of The Nightingale, after all these years."

"How do you know my name?" I asked. "I thought J. K. Priestley had only just managed to get the police evidence-files unlocked."

"News travels fast," he said. "Would you mind if I asked you a personal question?"

"You can't see the tattoo," I said, firmly. "Absolutely not."

"Actually, Mr. Ellsworth, that isn't what I was going to ask you. I understand about discretion, even though I've always been proud to show myself off. What I'd like to know, sir, if you'd consent to tell me, is whether you have bad dreams. The rest of us do, you see. Some of us are scared by them, but we're all anxious to discover whether there's any meaning in them."

I felt uneasy, remembering all too clearly what Melanie Millward had said about the lunatic fringe, and how there were people in the world who thought that Devon Curtin really had had *powers*. The fact that The Tree of the Knowledge of Good and Evil seemed to be stalking the ex-receptionist added plausibility to the hypothesis that he might indeed have lunatic tendencies. I knew that conventional advice counsels humoring lunatics, but I wasn't in the mood. "It's none of your business," I said.

He seemed oddly satisfied with that answer, evidently taking it as an affirmative one in disguise. "Did she tell you that it isn't magic?" he asked.

I made no reply to that, but just stared at him.

"Because I wonder, sometimes, whether it might be," he added, "even though I've always tried hard to believe the opposite." He reached into the back pocket of his trousers then, and produced a crumpled business-card, which bore his name and described him, more elaborately than the legend on the van, as a landscape gardener, hedge-trimmer and patio-constructor. "I'll be very glad to tidy up your garden if you like, sir," he said, "but I'm not touting for work just now. If you want to talk about old times, the dreams, the Goddess, or anything else, give me a ring and we can meet for a drink. I'll introduce you to Kim and the others if you like, but if you'd prefer to keep it strictly between the two of us, I'll understand. We look innocuous while we've got our clothes on, but we've been knocking around these parts for a long time, and plenty of people know who we are. I know things you might want to know, though and maybe things you need to know. May I call you Crispin?"

"It's Cris," I said, semi-automatically.

Again he nodded his head in satisfaction, although I had only been issuing a reflexive correction, not really granting him permission to call me by my first name. "You're famous, in your own fashion, Cris," he said. "Much more so than me—and maybe more than you suspected yourself, unless you've been keeping up with the gossip and the speculation on the web. You might need to be alert, now that Mel's found you. Paparazzi will be peering over your fence, hoping to get a sight of you while you're undressing for bed. You'll be news, at least for a little while, and in the right circles."

"What, exactly, do you want, Mr. More?" I asked him, somewhat dumbfounded.

"I'm curious," he repeated, disingenuously. "Interested in Devon Curtin, in the exhibition, in myself. We all want to learn more about ourselves, don't we? I'd like to know exactly what Curtin thought he was doing to me, and exactly what he did that got him killed. It wasn't me who shot him, by the way—I'm assuming that it wasn't you either."

"No," I said, "it wasn't me."

"Then you'll likely be as interested as I am in finding out—not so much the who as the why. If I had to bet, I'd plump for someone who had bad dreams, wouldn't you? Even if it isn't magic, there are definitely some who believed that it was—and just because you're paranoid, it doesn't mean that you haven't been cursed."

"Cursed?"

"Don't play the innocent, Cris—it must have crossed your mind. I think The Goddess thought she'd been cursed, although she never told me so in so many words—that's presumably why she left the country in such a hurry. The Falling Angel is more than half-convinced. We men don't admit such things as easily as the women, of course, but...well, it's certainly crossed my mind." His eyes, unmet by mine, strayed over the garden and the house again, as if to imply that anyone living in such an ill-kept place *had* to be cursed. *Curse*, I remembered, was one of the terms that Melanie Millward had suggested I combine with Devon Curtin's name if I wanted a short cut to the lunatic fringe, via Google.

I looked down at the card, feigning respectful interest. "If there's anything I need to know, or if I decide to finance a rescue mission for the rhododendrons," I said, "I'll be sure to give you a call."

"Or even if you just want a chat. I'm based in Hounslow, but I don't mind driving out here. I drive around all over the place, because of my job, and there are a lot more nice gardens along the westward reach of the Thames Valley than there are between Heathrow and the Hammersmith flyover. I'd certainly be interested in having a leisurely chat with The Nightingale, even if it turns out that you can't tell me anything I don't already know."

Stanley More cleared a lock of rain-soaked hair from his forehead and turned to go, in a hesitant manner suggestive of the belief, or hope, that I might ask him not to. I didn't. I was too confused.

He had already taken a couple of strides along the driveway when he half-turned, and said: "If you know where The Rose is, you really ought to give her the heads-up. If Mel gets to her first, she'll likely be snared before she's had time to think—and you might have something to say about that."

He didn't wait for any kind of response.

"These things come in threes," I muttered, as I closed the door again. "That'll be it for the time being, then."

I went back to work, and contrived to put in the hours I needed to get back on schedule, even though I was cruising on automatic, paying no real attention to what I was doing. When I had knocked off and checked my email, I moved swiftly on to the internet, figuring that I really ought to probe a little deeper into Devon Curtin's lunatic fringe.

Melanie Millward's suggestions were sound; combining Curtin's name with "magic" and "curse" produced a lot of hits. There seemed to be almost as many people who believed that tattoos in general, and his in particular, really did constitute a kind of magic, as there were who believed that it constituted Fine Art. Maybe things would have been slightly different if Curtin had still been alive, available for interview, or even if he'd ever got around to writing the book that Melanie had mentioned in the annex to the studio—but he was dead, having been shot by an unknown murderer, and everyone was perfectly free to speculate about what he might have thought about his work, or secretly tried to do by means of it.

When I added "Goddess" to the key words, the lunacy of the fringe intensified further, although it didn't take me long to realize that nobody actually knew anything at all. Apparently, as Stanley More had told me, she was rumored to have believed that she was under some kind of curse, and had therefore deemed it politic after Curtin's death to flee the country—but it was just rumor, plucked out of thin air. Exactly what the curse in question was supposed to have been, or why Devon Curtin should have wanted to inflict it upon her, was anyone's guess. One fantasist speculated that she really had been an object of worship for Curtin, and that it was actually a rival tattooist who had cursed her, lest she and he become too powerful in their magical association. Another suggested that he had betrayed her by screwing someone else—probably his receptionist and successor—and that she had tried to curse him, but that, as often happened when attempts at black magic were inexpertly made, the curse had rebounded on its sender. A third suggested that it was the unknown patron who had paid for Armina Holliman's work who had cursed her, because she had betrayed him by sleeping with Curtin, and that the same curse had led to Curtin's death, whether or not the cuckold had actually fired the shot.

Trying more elaborate combinations of keywords informed me that some interested parties, at least, had drawn connections between The Goddess's curse and The Nightingale and the Rose. One fantasist hypothesized that the dual tattoo, which required its possessors to be making love if its magic were to be activated and effective, was an instrument of the curse. Another suggested that it was actually an attempt to lift the curse. Everyone who had a hypothesis, however, seemed to assume that The Nightingale and the Rose was incomplete in more senses than one—that it was not merely fractured but that it had never been properly brought to fruition.

Oh shit, I thought. *Well, at least these crazies are only hypothetically interested in getting us back together, so that we can work the Tantric sex-oracle…if there is such a thing as a Tantric sex-oracle. How much worse would it be if they wanted us dead?*

There was only slightly more information about Stanley More on non-Curtin-associated websites than was inscribed on his business card, but there were plenty of pictures on Curtin-related sites of his tattoo, which covered his entire back. It was a slightly stylized tree, with fruits like acorns, although its leaves didn't seem to be shaped like an oak's. I couldn't see anything about the design that lent itself readily to the interpretation contained in its title: there was no serpent in its branches, so far as I could tell from the photographs, although I figured that far more detail might be visible if I were to see it in the flesh. I was in no hurry to do that.

I looked up some more images from the gallery of Curtin's supposedly minor works. There was more than one serpent there, including an anaconda and a cobra, as well as a couple of long-tailed and scaly-winged dragons. There was also a "reversed mermaid", with a fish's forequarters and a woman's nether regions, but little else in the way of cryptozoology. There were a couple of open books with pages covered in enigmatic hieroglyphics, and numerous items of jewelry, some of whose mountings looked more like armor than ornamentation.

I went back to the major works, especially the abundant representations of Armina Holliman. I couldn't see anything in her adornment, or the rest of the gallery, that entitled Curtin to be considered a genius, let alone a sorcerer capable of putting spells or curses on his human canvases, but I couldn't lay claim to any expertise in evaluating tattoos, either as art or as magic.

I knew, though, that I was going to have bad dreams, no matter what I cooked for dinner. In the event, I took a piece of battered cod out of the box in the freezer and put it in the oven, along with a tray of oven chips, and heated up some peas in the microwave. Then I watched TV for a couple of hours, without really paying attention. The ten o'clock news seemed to put things back into perspective somewhat. There were volcanoes threatening to erupt in Iceland and Kamchatka, perhaps violently enough to ground all air traffic in the northern hemisphere. Somali pirates had seized two more ships, one of them after a gun battle in which a number of crewmen on an oil tanker were believed to have been killed. The stock market had taken yet another dive in search of a record low for the twenty-first century. All in all, the popular prophecies of apocalypse in 2012 were looking more plausible with every passing day. Exhibitions of eccentric modern art were utterly irrelevant to anyone not directly involved.

When I went to bed, however—long after darkness had fallen, given that we were so close to the equinox—Luscinia stirred, and her song became more insistent. I honestly couldn't tell whether it was dream or delirium, or whether the distinction mattered any more, or whether it was madness or magic, or whether that was anything but a distinction without a difference. I did my best to lie back and endure it, reminding myself repeatedly that the pain was entirely imaginary, and that my eyes and heart were not being impaled in any authentic sense—but the reminders only added a sarcastic refrain to the song, which kept fading away and then surging forth again, both sweet and deadly, vital and fatal, soft and shrill.

The world of my dreams was overfull of roses: not merely Claire but also Melanie, both at somewhere around twenty and somewhere around forty, and Liz, in her younger days, and Karen, in hers. I didn't imagine myself erotically entwined with them all, mercifully, but they were all white roses, all thirsty for blood. If there was a tree of knowledge there, I couldn't find it, and I caught no more than fugitive glances of elusive forms that might have been aspects or avatars of The Goddess.

It's easy to become obsessive by night, when sleep is so shallow as to be imperceptible and trains of thought readily jump the track of rationality to crash through the wilderness of illogic, but I didn't feel that I was under any kind of curse. If I was paranoid, my paranoia was taking other and subtler forms.

When dawn broke, however—early, because the clocks hadn't yet gone forward to usher in British Summer Time—and my calm of mind was more-or-less restored, I started to draw out the argument I'd put to Melanie Millward, apparently before she could put it to me. It *was* only natural that the imagery of tattoos should permeate the wearer's dreams, by virtue of their common connection with the mysteries of the unconscious. Even if they didn't share the same source, that connection would be forged retrospectively, as a tattoo became a key symbolic referent for the unconscious to do its dream-work: dream-work that was magical in essence, even if it had no effect on recalcitrant reality. Even if it were just empty ritual, devoid of true meaning as well as tangible consequence, dream-work was an attempt by the human imagination to impose itself on the patterns of experience, the fabric of the inner life. There was a sense in which I really was The Nightingale now, even though no such idea had ever entered or exited my head before I had walked into The Artificial Paradise on that June afternoon twenty years before. Luscinia and I were more tightly bound together than any lovers, any father and daughter, any set of conjoined twins. We were the same person, even though I was a he and she was a she, I a real man and she a figurative bird. Her song was my song, her torment my torment; there was no point or plane at which she stopped and I began.

How I longed to fly! How I longed to be free! How claustrophobic it was to be trapped, to be wrapped around and stabbed by thorns!

Before I roused myself entirely from the grip of weariness and went to take a shower, I asked myself all the key questions again, and a few more besides.

If Armina Holliman was the girl in Wilde's story, who was the student? Surely it couldn't be Devon Curtin, because it wasn't the student who had given the girl the diamonds, as Curtin had clearly given the Goddess hers.

Why had The Nightingale and the Rose been designed and executed after the decoration of The Goddess, when the sacrifice was presumably already doomed to be futile, given her adornment with gems? Maybe because Curtin was trying to rewrite a story he'd already started, producing a revised draft.

If I really was The Nightingale, why wasn't I dead? Perhaps I *was* dead, metaphorically and symbolically speaking, even though my heart hadn't yet suffered its final shock and ceased to bleed.

Where was Claire now, and might she consent to lie beneath me, after all this time, to provide a simulation of love-making for the edification and amusement of Karen's school-friends? Would her tattoo—or mine, for that matter—ever truly reach artistic completion until we actually did make love, in true and heartfelt fashion, thus displaying the work of art as it was really meant to be displayed? Was Devon Curtin's murder a mere act of madness and misapprehension, or something more sinister?

There were far more questions than hypothetical answers, of course, and there was no science that could help me unravel the knot binding truth and fancy together.

But I am in pain, I thought, as I dried myself off and slowly got dressed, *and I do need to get out of it. If I can find a symbolic path, a ritual sequence of moves, my subtle mind might work the trick, whether or not I imagine it as magic....*

CHAPTER SEVEN

I'd had quite enough of callers who didn't take the trouble to telephone first to say that they were coming, so it was quite a relief when the phone rang, not long after ten-thirty on Friday morning had come and quietly gone. I picked up the extension on my desk in the study and said: "Hello."

"Cris," said a female voice. "Is that you?"

"Yes," I said, and waited for her to tell me who she was. Apparently, though, she had assumed that I would recognize her voice.

"How are you?" she asked.

"As well as can be expected," I replied, cautiously. "Who is this?"

"It's Claire," she informed me. It was as if someone had unexpectedly put a hand on my shoulder. I was momentarily paralyzed. Time seemed to stop—but it couldn't really have stopped, because she was obviously aware of the pause, and its pregnancy. Uncertainly, she added: "I used to be Claire Selvedge." Then she continued, in something of a rush: "Apparently, people are looking for me. There's going to be an exhibition of work by that tattooist we went to when we were high after finishing finals, when we thought we were in love. They seem to be looking for you—but you're not hard to find, with the aid of Google and Directory Enquiries. Have they been in touch with you yet?"

My mind filled up with images and thoughts of Claire, seemingly becoming jammed. I had expected the moment to come, of course, ever since I'd spoken to J. K. Priestley, but the manner of its arrival was so unexpected that I was shocked into dire confusion. "Yes," I said, when I contrived to activate my vocal cords. "They've hired a private detective to find you, but I don't think my phone's tapped, so there's probably nothing to worry about."

"It's only a matter of time," she said, resignedly. "I'm not in hiding, or abroad. Once they have my married name, it'll be child's play."

"You're married, then?" I said, warily.

"Divorced—but I didn't go back to my maiden name. You?"

"The same—divorced, that is." Foolishly, I added: "I didn't have a maiden name not to go back to." I cursed myself for my awkwardness.

"How long ago?" Her voice seemed more assured, but I guessed that it was an illusion of technology. She had as little idea of what to say as I did, and was fishing for platitudes.

"Oh a long time now—thirteen years, give or take a few months. I'm still in touch with my daughter, though. She's seventeen. Do you have kids?"

"Not any more. My son died. Childhood leukemia."

"Oh—I'm sorry."

"It was a while ago now," she said, although the telephonic mask couldn't conceal the dissimulation in the statement. "Six years. He was nine." She paused, then continued, in an awkwardly plaintive fashion: "Sometimes, though, I really do feel like a bloodstained rose, blighted and spoiled. The marriage couldn't survive it. He's married again, now. I haven't been able to. One thing and another."

It seemed to me that she was casting about for a kind of intimacy that we didn't really have—that we had never really had. I sympathized, and wished that I had an appropriate response ready, emotionally as well as verbally. "Why did you track me down, Claire?" I asked, uncertainly. "If it's about the exhibition…."

"Of course it's about the exhibition," she interrupted, too immediately dismissive of the suggestion that she might have any other motive. "Have they been in touch? What did you say to them?"

"Yes," I said, "and no."

It took her a moment or two to figure it out, but she got there. "You're living in Maidenhead," she said. It was a statement, not a question. She must have found that out somehow, before calling a directory enquiry number. Obviously, the internet really was in the process of abolishing privacy.

"Yes."

"I'm in Farnham. Do you drive?"

"No. I never had any need, and couldn't be bothered to learn."

"Do you mind if I come to you, then. Is there a convenient place where we can meet? I've never actually been to Maidenhead. I'd prefer a café or coffee-shop to a pub, if that's okay. We really ought to talk—to figure out what we're going to do."

She seemed to be taking it for granted that I would leap at the chance to meet—to discuss the threat of the exhibition, of course, and to come to an agreement as to how we were going to handle it. We were, after all, two halves of a single work of art.

Three days before, I wouldn't have been sure about leaping at a chance to meet, but a lot had happened in the previous fifty hours. "There's a Starbuck's in the High Street," I said. "You'll have to pay to park in one of the multi-stories, but if we're paying that much for a cup of coffee, what's a few quid to park the car?"

"I think I can afford it," she said. "Can you get there for twelve-thirty?"

"Yes, easily."

"I'll see you there, then." She still seemed to be in a hurry. Given that J. K. Priestley or Melanie Millward might come knocking on her door at any moment, armed with promises of cash or threats of nudity, she was probably justified in her anxiety, and grateful for a chance to get out of the neighborhood. Farnham was by no means a million miles away from London.

She rang off without saying goodbye, or thank you, or telling me how good it was to hear my voice again. Perhaps it wasn't. Hearing hers had virtually paralyzed me, and the effect still hadn't cleared—but that, too, was an effect of the particular circumstances. I'd already psyched myself up to be gladdened by the prospect of making contact with her again, and when the temporary paralysis did wear off, the gladness dutifully made its entrance.

I concentrated hard, remembering her as she'd been at twenty: delicate but firm, bright and steadfast, as pure as a cloudless sky and as soft as...well, softness itself. I also remembered me as I'd been at twenty, because I couldn't help it: awkward and incompetent in spite of my intellectual arrogance, cursed with the wrong reflexes. No wonder it had all gone awry

I tidied myself up before leaving the house, putting on my best jacket but stopping short of donning a tie. The weather was cloudy again, but there was no immediate threat of rain. It was slightly colder than I'd expected, given global warming, but not too uncomfortable without a pullover. I set off at a brisk walk, with the same enthusiastic stride I had used when I went to catch the bus to Bracknell, in the days before Karen grew old enough not to require collection.

I got to the shop ten minutes early, ordered a latte and took possession of a table for two, knowing that the lunch-time rush might start at any moment. By the time Claire arrived, five minutes late, the seat opposite mine was the last one untaken. I had already switched off my mobile phone, armoring myself against any possible interruption by the enemy.

Chivalrously, I stood up. I didn't tower over her the way I once had; my slightly stooped posture and her high heels reduced the margin from four inches to somewhere between two and three. She was still slender, but not as willowy as she had been at twenty. She was still blonde, although I had the impression that the color was chemically enhanced. Her eyes were still blue, but not as clear or bright as I remembered them. Her skin was still pale, but had lost its near-luminous sheen. She was still beautiful, but tangibly careworn.

Doubtless she was taking similar inventory of me. I didn't doubt that the measurement she made of my deterioration would be considerably greater than the one I made of hers. She tried to smile, but only half-succeeded. I told her how good it was to see her again, but it sounded like an empty ritual remark. She only nodded, but she seemed grateful to be there—and curious too.

I invited her to sit down, and went to order her a coffee. She asked for a double espresso, which suggested that she didn't feel that she was sufficiently strong to tackle the encounter without a chemical boost.

As I brought the coffees back to the table I made a more general appraisal of her appearance. Like Melanie Millward, Claire had aged relatively gracefully, and respectably. She was wearing a neat beige jacket and a pale blue blouse. It wasn't obvious that either of us was a work of art, and certainly not that we were two components of a single work of art executed by a tattooist inspired by the unsatisfied spirit of Edgar Allan Poe. We probably looked to an unwary observer like a small businessman and his secretary-cum-lover contriving a secret meeting away from the office—not in the least out of place in a High Street coffee shop.

"It's been a long time," I observed, mildly, hoping that she wouldn't say "Not long enough."

She didn't. "It's strange," she said, "knowing that people are looking for me, and bound to find me before much longer, for such a peculiar reason. You didn't mind me calling, I hope?"

"No," I said.

"And you said no—to them, I mean. You told them that you didn't want to appear in their exhibition?"

"Yes—but they're very reluctant to take no for an answer. Melanie—do you remember Melanie, the receptionist?—seemed to think that you'd be bound to agree, and that your agreement would secure mine. She couldn't seem to understand why I'd refused so promptly or so adamantly. She thinks it's a great opportunity, which any sane person would seize."

Claire's blue eyes were staring at me, seemingly frankly. "It would be a bit embarrassing," she remarked—which hardly seemed like a ringing endorsement of my committed and principled position.

"They want us to pose lying down in the missionary position," I told her. "If we won't agree to do it live, they want to film us—or, failing that, take a series of still photographs in the relevant position."

"If that would satisfy them...." she began—but she didn't finish the sentence, apparently uncertain as to whether she should have started it.

"Do you have bad dreams?" I asked her, bluntly. "Dreams involving the tattoo?"

The question didn't faze or amaze her. "Of course I do," she said. "Don't you?"

"Yes," I said.

"It's only natural," she told me. "After the murder…and it's always there, whenever I stand naked. I don't even need a mirror to see it. Sometimes, I think it's more me than I am. Of course I dream about it—and yours too."

"You dream about nightingales?"

She blushed. "Yes," she said, briefly, evidently not about to discuss the precise contents of her nightingale-featuring dreams. "It should all have faded away long ago, I suppose, but some things never do, do they? I still think about you sometimes. You were my first, you know. Whenever I look back…."

"Yes, I know," I said. "You're unassailably enshrined in my memory too. It was a significant rite of passage, even if it all went awry. Even if we didn't have the tattoos to provide constant reminders….."

"I suppose so. How could we possibly have imagined that, in twenty years' time, people would actually be looking for us, wanting to put us on show? But they will settle for photographs, won't they? And they'll be willing to block out our heads, so we wouldn't be recognizable."

"Our names are known, Claire. Mine will probably be on the internet by the time I get home. At present, they only have your maiden name, but it's a matter of days now—maybe hours. We can't hope to remain anonymous. Even so, you're probably right. If we provide a few photographs, that will cool the frenzy, take the core out of the mystery. Melanie and her curator will settle for that, I think…although there seem to be other people interested, who might continue to pester us."

"What other people?"

"I've only met a landscape gardener called Stanley More, but he might be the tip of the iceberg. The prospect of the exhibition seems to have started a snowball rolling, and it's gathering mass as well as pace. There's been mention of paparazzi, and Curtin's fan club has a lunatic fringe. The threat might be exaggerated, but it might not. If and when the exhibition actually opens, at the end of June…."

"I see," she said. "God, what idiots we were."

"To fall in love, or to fall out of it again so quickly?" I queried.

"To get the stupid tattoos. It was my fault, I know. You'd never have put them on your credit card if you hadn't been so intent on impressing me, and I hadn't been so intent on letting you. I was in a manic mood. I didn't give you much choice, in the circumstances, did I?"

"As I remember," I said, scrupulously, "it was my idea to go into the shop."

"And as I remember," she countered, "it was my idea to drop the Es."

"It wasn't the Es," I told her. "They'd worn off. It wasn't even the intoxication of mutual infatuation. We knew what we were doing. It really did seem like a good idea at the time. According to Melanie, it was, and we ought to be extremely grateful for our stroke of good luck. We're a work of art now—one that's on the brink of being declared to be important by people who really matter. This time next year, we might be deemed a work of genius, like *Guernica* or the Sistine Chapel ceiling."

"More like Tracy Emin's bed," she said, "or that tent with the names of all the people she'd ever slept with. Better that, I suppose, than a pickled shark or something with elephant dung."

"So what do you want us to do about it, if we're to present a united front?" I asked. "We've stolen a march on them, I think, by getting together before they could work on you separately. In fact, it might be a good idea for us to call them, preemptively, rather than waiting for them to find you. If we stick together, we can probably force our decision on them, rather than giving them space to come between us."

"I thought sticking together was exactly what they want us to do," she remarked, in jest, proving that the double espresso hadn't strung her out too far. "How do you feel about it? Is posing for a few photographs the lesser of two evils—or the least of three?"

"Probably, if you feel up to it."

I winced as soon as the words were out of my mouth, seeing the set up for the *double entendre*—but if she noticed it, she let it alone. "It's not that big a deal," she said. "I'm not an ingénue, after all, and there's no point in trying to resurrect my maidenly modesty. It's not as if you haven't lain on top of me before, or there wouldn't *be* a work of art. I'm well over the break-up, and I presume you are too."

"Sure," I said. "If you sound that blasé about it when you talk to Melanie Millward, though, she'll scent blood and come after us like a rottweiler, trying to persuade us to do the live show. She threatened to strip naked in my living room in order to bully me into taking my shirt off."

"Why didn't you let her?" Claire enquired. "It doesn't sound like much of a threat to me. What was so horrible about the prospect of seeing her naked?"

It was a good question. I wondered why it hadn't occurred to me before. I shrugged my shoulders. "I guess you had to be there," I said, weakly.

"Next time, I probably will be. Have we reached an agreement or are we still debating? If we have, we ought to plan the next step, don't you think?"

"You seem to be in a hurry," I observed.

"We're working against the clock," she reminded me. "If we're trying to take the initiative, there's no such thing as too soon."

I shrugged again, and took out my mobile. I had to ferret around for the card with J. K. Priestley's number on it, but it only took a few seconds.

"Photographs," I said, before dialing. "Stills only. At home, or in a studio. If at home, yours or mine?"

"Home," she said. "Personally, I'd prefer yours. They might not have found out where I live yet, and it would be nice if we could put an end to the search before they track me down. Unless there's a problem—you have a daughter, you said?"

"Karen's no problem," I assured her. "She lives with her mother—and all she said when I told her about my being asked to take part in the exhibition was 'Cool.' She threatened to get her school to arrange a trip to the gallery, so all our friends could see us. She'll probably be disappointed if we're only there in photographs, with our faces deliberately obscured. Shall I dial?"

"Go ahead."

I punched out the number of J. K. Priestley's office. A secretary answered, but when I gave her my name she put me straight through.

I didn't waste any time. "I've located Claire," I said. "She's sitting with me now. We're prepared to pose for still photographs at my house. You can send a professional photographer, but we'd rather not have a crowd. We want to be as discreet as possible, while giving you something to exhibit."

"Can we fix something up for tomorrow?" he asked, without any preamble.

I checked with Claire, then said: "Yes. Any time you like."

"Ten-thirty A.M," he said.

I agreed.

When I'd put the phone away, I said: "Would you like to see the house and help pick a location? Forewarned is forearmed. It's only ten minutes' walk, but if you bring the car, you can make a quick getaway. You can park in the driveway."

"All right," she said. She picked up her handbag instantly, still operating in top gear. Her double espresso had gone, but I had to finish up the remains of my latte in a hurry. It was still hot; things were moving fast.

As we left the shop, I saw Stanley More standing on the other side of the road, not even trying to hide. He didn't wave, but he might actually have winked. He didn't follow us back to the multi-storey car park either, but that was presumably because he already knew what he wanted to know. He knew that I'd found The Rose—or that The Rose had found me.

I didn't point him out to Claire, or tell her that he was there. I figured that he was my problem, for the time being, if he was a problem at all.

CHAPTER EIGHT

When we got back to the house, Karen was sitting on the doorstep. She was wearing her school uniform, and it was the middle of the day, so I immediately assumed that she was playing truant. She assured me that she wasn't, insisting that her class had been allowed to leave school early for lack of a supply teacher to cover her English teacher's absence, the pupils having been advised to devote themselves to revision.

"Stress," she said, to explain the teacher's absence, while she eyed Claire up and down, curiously. "There's a lot of it about. You sounded a bit stressed yourself when you phoned yesterday, so I thought I'd take advantage of the opportunity before I went home to Mum. What she doesn't know won't annoy her."

"My daughter Karen," I said to Claire. "This is Claire," I said to Karen, unable to add a surname.

"*The* Claire?" Karen asked, only slightly surprised. I had told her enough on the phone to establish a context of expectation for the revelation.

Claire looked at me, clearly wondering how much I'd told me daughter about my tattoo, and my pre-marital adventures. "The one and only," I said, as I unlocked the front door. For Claire's benefit, I added: "Karen knows the whole story. I don't have any secrets from her, although she never tells me anything." Even the latter part of the statement wasn't entirely true.

"Very wise," said Claire. "It's a father's duty to be an open book to his daughter, and a daughter's privilege to conceal her secrets from her father." It sounded painfully glib, coming from someone whose only child had died, at the cost of her marriage. It opened the door for Karen to speak to her in a similarly mock-confidential manner, however, and Karen didn't miss the opportunity.

"How on Earth did Dad find you?" she asked. "I didn't think he ever left the house any more, except to go to the shops, now that he doesn't have to come to Bracknell to collect me anymore. Detective work really isn't his thing—especially legwork."

"He didn't find me," Claire replied. "I found him. I'm still in hiding, but he was easy to locate. He isn't even ex-directory."

"I've warned him about the perennial danger of identity theft," Karen told her, with a contrived sigh, "but he doesn't listen."

"Who'd want my identity?" I muttered, as I stood aside to usher them into the hallway. I was talking to myself but—as usual, given that I usually had no one to overhear what I said to myself—I'd spoken too loudly.

"Don't knock yourself," Karen said, as she showed Claire into the sitting room. "If what I've recently been reading on the internet is reliable, you've quietly become a celebrity, in a mysterious sort of way. I never realized—I always took the thing for granted—but you're *The Nightingale*. The *missing* Nightingale, of which there isn't even a photograph. And now you're reunited with The Rose—how romantic can you get? Shall I make us all a spot of lunch? If you've got anything in the fridge, that is."

Only too well aware of the fridge situation, I said: "No need. I'll make us a cup of tea, though."

"I'll have coffee, if that's okay," Claire said. "Black and strong. Can I use your bathroom."

"I'll show you where it is," Karen volunteered.

I put the kettle on and made tea for Karen and myself, and strong black coffee for Claire. I put some fruit shortcake biscuits on a plate and carried the whole lot into the sitting room on a tray, feeling very civilized but wishing I'd taken Melanie Millward's hint and cleaned up a bit when I'd had the chance.

"So you're going to let them take photographs for the exhibition," Karen said, obviously having carried her interrogation of Claire a little further. "Surely not *here?*" It wasn't clear whether she meant the sitting room, or the whole house. I hadn't given the specifics much thought, as yet, but the politics of the situation abruptly loomed up, in all their awkwardness. There was, in fact, little or no scope for taking photographs in any of the downstairs rooms, even if one set aside the difficulties of posing. It would have to be done in one of the bedrooms. The necessity of tidying up and cleaning became even more urgent, and the prospects for embarrassment increased markedly. Perhaps, I thought, we should have opted for a photographic studio—and a longer delay.

"We'll have to give that some thought," I said. "I suppose you need your bus fare reimbursing."

"Yes please. I suppose I shouldn't hang around—you too must have a lot of catching up to do."

Claire and I both hastened to deny that, our insincere responses all the more inarticulate by virtue of overlapping.

"It seems there's not much left to discuss, then," Karen observed. "Still, it's good to see you, Dad—and I'm glad to have met you, Claire. I won't say that I've heard a lot about you, because that might sound ominous, and I certainly won't ask for a peek at your tattoo. I'll see the photographs when the exhibition opens, won't I?"

"You really don't have to go so soon," I said. "I only wanted to show Claire where the house is because we're meeting the people from the exhibition here tomorrow—although I'm no longer sure that we should do the photo shoot here. We just want to get the whole thing out of the way and get back to our lives in peace." It didn't sound convincing, even to me.

Karen looked at Claire, evidently suspicious of my entitlement to speak for both of us. Claire wouldn't meet her gaze. "That's not going to happen, Dad," she said, slowly. "You must at least have glanced at the websites. There's too much stored-up curiosity, and the people mounting the exhibition are trying to make as much capital out of it as they can. They may not be able to whip up a frenzy, but it won't end with taking a few photographs. Even if they agree to let you alone in return for posing, the curiosity won't go away. You're just thickening the plot, not providing a denouement." She didn't seem to be suffering overmuch from the absence of her English teacher—and it was obvious that she was right. It would have been obvious even if I hadn't seen Stanley More loitering in Maidenhead High Street, having presumably followed me to my rendez-vous with Claire.

"She's right, isn't she?" said Claire, echoing my own thought. "We can't stop the ball rolling."

"No, we can't," I admitted. "Melanie Millward has too much invested in this exhibition to let us off the hook that easily. Even if we refuse to take any further active part in her plans, she's going to milk the story of the reuniting of The Nightingale and The Rose for all it's worth. We really might get doorstepped by paparazzi, if her PR's any good. Shit. There's only one thing that can save us."

"Katla blowing her lid big-time?" Karen suggested, referring to the Icelandic volcano that was currently in the news. I didn't pause to wonder why she was thinking of the volcano as a female; I always tried not to think too hard about the effects her rampant hormones might be having on her body and behavior.

"Lydia the tattooed lady," I retorted, grimly. "The only thing that'll kill our story in its tracks is a bigger and better one—or, at least, a sexier one. If they can find Armina Holliman at just the right time...."

"Come off it, Dad," Karen said, with a blithe lack of diplomacy that only a seventeen-year-old could manifest. "What's sexier than the idea of you and Claire having it off in order to reactivate your art-work and renew its magic power?"

Claire's blush was all the more striking by virtue of her pale complexion.

"We aren't intending to go that far," I told her, bluntly. "Devon Curtin didn't require it of us when he marked us up for the tattoos, and we're certainly not going to turn tomorrow's photo shoot into a porn movie. We've agreed to pose—but that's all we've agreed to."

"I didn't mean that you were actually going to *do the deed*," Karen hastened to explain. "I only meant that that's what's on everybody's mind—well, not everybody, but the people that like to think of themselves as true connoisseurs of art. You *have* looked at the websites, haven't you?"

She was right again, infuriatingly. That kind of curiosity, once having been piqued, would only be intensified by half-measures. In fact, it couldn't ever be quieted at all, even by a blue movie or a live performance, given that any such performance, real or simulated, would always be open to criticism, always judged by an esthetic standard impossible to meet. The fact that we weren't twenty years old anymore, and that the aging process hadn't been extraordinarily kind to Claire, let alone to me, was only part of the problem, but it was more than sufficient in itself to ensure that Devon Curtin's supposed masterpiece never could be seen in the manner that it had been imagined in his mind's eye. The work of art, as he had conceived it, had been so ephemeral that it had never actually come into being, even momentarily and in private. Not only weren't we young and handsome any more, but we weren't in love...even if all that "in love" had meant back then had been a petty infatuation, enhanced by the lingering effects of a couple of Es.

"Unless, of course," Karen added, effortlessly maintaining her careless insouciance, "they also find that the mystery lady with all the tattoo bling was the one who shot the tattoo guy dead. That wouldn't actually be sexier, but it *would* be newsworthier. Is *newsworthier* actually a word?"

"They haven't even found her yet," I pointed out. "Finding out that she's a murderer at the same time would be a furlong too far in the coincidence stakes—besides which, it's hardly the sort of thing you should be wishing on someone. Anyway, she didn't do it—not according to Jakey Priestley."

"How does he know?" Karen wanted to know. I couldn't tell her.

"Your daughter's right," Claire said. "We do have a lot to talk about, Cris. We need to make plans—more elaborate and extensive plans than the one we threw together back at Starbuck's."

"You could flee the country," Karen suggested, unseriously. "Heathrow's just down the road. You really ought to spend more time in France, Dad." She knew that my spoken French was terrible, because all the translation I did was working from documents. I hadn't actually set foot in France since the early days of my ill-fated marriage.

"Yeah," I said. "That would really reduce our newsworthiness."

Karen smiled broadly.

"What are you grinning at?" I asked.

"The thought of Mum's face, when she finds out what's going on," she said. I didn't care enough to be amused by the thought myself.

"You can't blame her, Cris," Claire put in, leaping to an altogether unnecessary defense. "To her, this is all rather exciting—something to gossip about."

"I do *not* gossip," Karen said. "Mothers gossip, daughters merely take a healthy interest in the world around them. And I really don't want my Dad to get his knickers in a twist. I'd better go—not because I'm in a huff, but because I really oughtn't to be late home, or Mum will wonder where I've got to, and think the worst."

"Okay," I said. "Thanks for coming over. I really do appreciate it, even though we haven't had a chance to talk."

"We have been talking," she pointed out. "Nice to meet you, Claire—I hope it all works out for you, without too much hassle."

Claire thanked her kindly, and politely stayed in her seat while I showed Karen to the door. I gave her a goodbye hug, and thanked her again for responding to my cry for help, albeit a little belatedly. She tripped off down the driveway like someone who hadn't a care in the world, although she paused on her way past the bindweed-laden rhododendrons to appraise Claire's yellow Datsun, seemingly appreciatively. To her, it was all rather exciting. I wished that I could adopt the same attitude myself.

When I went back into the sitting room, I found Claire deep in thought, with a furrowed brow.

"You could still take the Heathrow option if you wanted to," I said, not really meaning it. "Unfortunately, the exhibition's still the best part of three months away. It's not really practicable to lie low until it's all over."

"Maybe we're getting too paranoid," she said, optimistically. "Maybe once they've taken the photographs, it will all go away. It's not really news, is it? They're just tattoos, for God's sake."

If only that were true, I thought. And it might have been true, if only I'd been a little more sensible, a little saner. Devon Curtin's receptionist had been right: I should never have named the nightingale Luscinia. In fact, I should never have named her at all. I should never have started identifying her with my pain, and I certainly shouldn't have appointed Luscinia as my patron saint and martyr, the receptacle for all my subsequent anguish and all my subsequent distress, to the point at which her imaginary song became unbearable and unavoidable. If only I'd struck the right mental attitude to start with, Curtin's design really could have been just a tattoo, of no particular existential consequence. All I could say aloud, though, was: "Are they?"

I could tell by the expression on her face that her rose was no mere pattern of ink in her own estimation. I couldn't believe that it had become the focal point of as many bad dreams as my own, but I couldn't believe that it had let her alone either.

"No," she admitted. "They're not. Not to me, anyway."

I sat down, heavily. "Do you believe in curses?" I asked.

"Of course I do. I'm not menopausal yet. If it hadn't been for the curse…."

That wasn't what I meant, of course, but the incomplete sentence hooked me anyway. "What do you mean?" I asked.

"If I hadn't been premenstrual," She said, "none of it would have happened—the Es, the sex, the break-up. I used to get really manic in those days, seriously unstable. The stress of finals and the impending results made it even worse. Surely you didn't think I was like that *all* the time? I tried to pick up the pieces afterwards, I really did—but it was all too much."

It was news to me; she certainly hadn't said anything at the time. My amazement must have been clearly legible in my expression, because she said: "Oh God, Cris—surely you haven't been thinking all these years that it was *your* fault?"

"It wasn't yours either," I hastened to say. "It doesn't change anything. We both knew what we were doing."

"Speak for yourself," she said. "To me, back then, it seemed as if something alien took me over for the best part of a week, steering in me in directions I would never have followed normally—and steering you too, in that particular instance. I'm truly sorry, Cris. I couldn't say so at the time, but…well, it's too late now, I know."

"You don't have anything to apologize for," I insisted. "If I hadn't been so awkward, and so intensely focused on trying to control my awkwardness, to overcome my touch taboo, to make a good impression….well, I'd probably have noticed that you were having difficulties too. Jesus, I hope…." I stopped.

"What?" she queried—and then guessed. "You hope Karen has an easier ride. She probably will. She's beautiful."

"*You* were beautiful," I pointed out. "It didn't seem to help."

"It's nice of you to say so…to think so," she said, although the use of the past tense must have needled her slightly, "but I wasn't really beautiful. Your daughter is."

"We're both prejudiced by lack of self-confidence," I said, "but you and I have the testimony of at least two objective observers. Melanie Millward thought we were both beautiful—she said so in so many words, only yesterday—and so did Devon Curtin."

"He told me that it was just the pallor of my skin." Her tone was reflective. "Color was his thing, he said, not love."

I remembered that he's said exactly the same thing to me. That wasn't surprising. Much of what he'd said must have been oft-repeated patter, far too routinized to have been part of any more sinister ritual. I couldn't believe that the tattooist had believed, even for a single second, that there was any actual magic in what he was doing, let alone that he was in the process of casting some kind of arcane spell or lifting some kind of curse. Claire and I—and all the other illustrated people who suffered from bad dreams—were victims of our own delusions, our own self-dissatisfactions. We had all cursed ourselves, or brought imaginary curses down upon our own stupid heads.

"I'd better give you the tour," I said, when the reflective pause seemed to have gone on long enough. "We need to figure out where the photographs ought to be taken—and how we're going to go on from there." I stood up again.

She stood up too, rather wearily. "Would it have been any better, do you think," she said, "if we'd stayed together, at least for a while longer? If we really had enacted the work of art as Curtin envisaged it? We never really *made love* again, did we, after that first hectic time?"

"It would be better if he'd managed to take the photographs himself, as he intended," I said, dodging the issue. "If any photographs already existed, Melanie and the curator probably wouldn't have bothered to track us down—or, at least, would have accepted our refusal to appear in the flesh with a modicum of grace."

She made a slight grimace, and I realized that she was no longer much concerned about our present predicament. She'd moved on to deeper questions, and they were troubling her. I knew then that the extent of her disenchantment, whether or not it was as great as my own, was far from trivial. Her marriage had worked out considerably worse than mine; her child had died. She had more right to consider herself cursed than I did, and more cause to wonder whether she might have done better to take a different path in life at a much earlier stage. I'd always thought of myself as a lost soul, condemned to a peculiar purgatory, but I knew as I looked at Claire, standing there with her head bowed, four inches shorter than me once again, in spite of her high heels, that I'd been self-indulgent in my misery.

I wanted to put my arm around her to comfort her, but I couldn't. The only person in the world that I could put my arm around without first mustering the most fervent concentration was Karen.

I showed Claire the second spare bedroom that wasn't ever used as a bedroom, because no one ever stayed over except Karen. "I'll move out most of the clutter tonight," I said "I'll clean round as well. I think I can have everything looking respectable by ten-thirty."

"Not everything," she said, speaking to herself but pronouncing the words too loudly, by force of the same habit I'd acquired, presumably having acquired it the same way.

I didn't try to reassure her that she looked fine, although she did; she might, after all, be thinking about me rather than herself. Before I could say anything at all, in fact, she said: "I'll give you a hand. It's only fair. I was the one who wanted to do the shoot here, because I was still trying to protect my own hidey-hole from God knows what."

CHAPTER NINE

It was nearly seven o'clock when Claire finally left to drive back to Farnham. She still hadn't told me her current surname, or her address, but she had programmed the number of her mobile into mine. I still hadn't plucked up the courage to put my arm around her, or make any other physical approach, so we bid one another farewell without so much as a handshake.

I was hungry, having skipped lunch, but not hungry enough to deflect me from my intention. I watched the Datsun until it disappeared around the corner, and then watched the gap at the end of the driveway for a few moments, half-expecting to see some other vehicle—probably a white van—glide past in furtive pursuit. None did. Then I went back into the house, switched my mobile phone back on, and called Stanley More, without even bothering to check my voicemail first.

He answered on the second ring. "More Landscaping," he said.

"Mr. More? It's Cris Ellsworth."

"Hey! I've been trying to ring you, but your phone went straight to voicemail. Where the hell are you?"

"Don't you know? I thought you were following me."

"Better things to do, mate. Where did you say you were?"

"I'm at home," I snapped, annoyed by his insouciance. "Where are you?"

"In the van, driving westwards on the M4. Can't talk for long—don't have a hands-free set. Got to respect the law—can't afford to lose my license. I'm glad you're home; I'm not far away, in that case. I was going to stop by in any case, hoping to pick you up. I need you to do me a big favor."

"Why the hell should I do any favors for you?" I demanded.

"Why the hell shouldn't you? You called me, didn't you? Better late than never. Perhaps I should have said that I'm in a position to do *you* a favor, knowledge-wise—but if you want to haggle, I'll gladly give you a big discount on tidying up your garden, starting tomorrow if you like. As I said, can't talk now—I'll be there in fifteen, maybe twenty."

"Stopping by on the way to where?" I asked

"You'll see when we get there. Bye." He cut the connection.

I almost rang back, to demand some answers, but there didn't seem to be much point, given that I'd be able to put the questions to him face to face in less than half an hour. I used the spare time to make and consume a corned beef sandwich, washed down with summer-fruit squash.

He didn't get out of the van when he pulled up in the driveway, but simply tooted his horn. I went out and opened the door on the passenger side. Like many vans, it had a long front seat capable of accommodating two seat-belted passengers as well as the driver. The position next to him was already occupied by an exceedingly buxom woman in her forties. I looked at her uncertainly.

"This is Kim Connor," said Stanley More. "Kim, this is Cris Ellsworth, alias The Nightingale. You probably know Kim as The Falling Angel, Cris. We were having a chat when things started happening."

Kim certainly didn't look like an angel, nor did she look, any longer, like a body-builder. The muscles she'd cultivated in the days when Devon Curtin had tattooed her had all turned to fat, and then some. Her inky Angel might still be Falling, but she gave the impression that she'd hit rock bottom quite some time ago. Comparing her present bulk with the photographs on the internet, I judged that Devon Curtin's tattoo must have been stretched almost to the point of caricature since he'd applied the ink. Her face wasn't unpleasant, though. She had strangely child-like features. Although my expertise at reading expressions left something to be desired, I thought that she was looking at me fondly, perhaps even with a hint of lust. I tried to take it as a compliment, although I knew that my false reputation as The Nightingale had gone before me, perhaps writing imaginary checks that the real me couldn't begin to cash.

"Come on!" said More, impatiently.

I climbed up beside The Falling Angel and hastily engaged my seat belt as he backed up rapidly on to the road. "Can't hang about," he said. "Racing the detectives. How did you find the Rose?"

"I didn't," I said. "She rang me—she didn't have anyone else to talk to."

"Snap."

"What do you mean, *snap*?"

"I mean the same thing happened to me. She rang me because she didn't have anyone else to talk to—and found Kim too. Neat, hey? One of those coincidences that makes you feel that fate's on your side, that the Force is with you, or whatever."

"Claire rang you too?" I said, wonderingly.

"No—keep up, will you. *Armina* rang me. She's been back in the country for a couple of days, apparently—packed her bags and booked a flight when she saw the news about the exhibition. She's obviously treading warily, though—didn't want to make contact with Mel right away, without scouting out the lie of the land. I'm even easier to locate than you are—I come up right away on Google, in spite of the fact that my name's not nearly as uncommon as yours, provided that you type in 'gardener' as well. She remembered me fondly from the old days, of course. She knows I'm a man who knows things, so I'm the one she called. Just wait till I actually turn up with The Nightingale! It's as well that I got hold of you, though; I'd promised, and I'd look a bit of a fool if I turned up without the goods—meaning no disrespect to you, Kim."

"No offense taken," The Falling Angel assured him.

"You promised Armina Holliman that you'd bring me to meet her?" I said, not at all sure that I was keeping up. "Did she ask you to do that?"

"Not in so many words—but she did ask whether Mel had found you. She surfs the net too, you know—easy enough, whether she's been in America, Hong Kong or Timbuktu. She didn't say."

"Why would she want to see me?" I asked, guardedly.

"Any number of reasons—as I'm sure you must know, if you've been surfing yourself. Maybe just because she was Devon Curtin's number one fan—not in a Kathy Bates kind of way, of course—and she'd be as tickled pink as any of the others to find one of his lost works. You're the solution to one of his little mysteries, aren't you? I don't suppose there's any chance of picking up The Rose too? Where's she living nowadays."

Farnham was way back in the wrong direction, so there seemed no point in telling him even that much. We were already on the slip road leading to the westbound carriageway of the M4. I touched the mobile phone in my pocket, but I didn't want to ring Claire while I had every reason to think that she was in her car. I had to suppose that she would be interested in the turn that events had just taken, but I figured that I'd be able to bring her up to date in the morning, when I'd found out what it was all about myself.

"It's not on the way," I told Stanley More. "Where, exactly, are we going?"

"Only as far as Reading," he said. "She took the Railair coach from Heathrow, and got a room in the Renaissance. Personally, I'd have settled for the Ibis, but they hadn't built that last time she was in these parts. She probably still thinks of the Renaissance as the Ramada. A bit conspicuous, mind, if she's really trying to lie low. I expect that she just wants to check up on how things stand before making her approach to Mel. Can't be short of a bob or two if she's staying at a place like that, but I don't suppose for a minute that it's the prospect of a fee that brought her back."

"You *were* following me earlier, weren't you?" I said. "You followed me to Starbuck's. Why?"

"Because I didn't want to hang about outside the detective agency's offices, given that I didn't suppose for a minute they'd be doing any actual legwork. I figured that I'd lit enough of a fire under your tail to set you going, and that you might lead me to The Rose. I was right, wasn't I?"

"You're flattering yourself," I assured him. "If Claire hadn't called, I'd have sat at home all day, twiddling my thumbs, because I wouldn't have known where to start with what you call legwork. You were just lucky."

"Bully for me, then. Now I've got the holy hat-trick: The Nightingale, The Rose *and* The Goddess."

"You haven't *got* anyone," I said, acidly. "I'm not even convinced that you actually *know* anything about anything, in spite of all the hints you keep dropping. I suspect that you're just a clown who likes playing games, and hasn't got enough gardening work to keep him busy, because it's only March and nothing's really started growing yet."

"You'd be surprised what's started growing," he retorted. "I knew about your bad dreams, didn't I? The Rose has them too, doesn't she? It's not true that all dog-owners end up looking like their pets, but it *is* true that all people with tattoos are possessed, in a manner of speaking. I'll bet that Armina has had some fascinating dreams in the last twenty years. She's a victim, like the rest of us, in spite of her title. She might be in search of someone to lift the curse that she thinks Devon put on her. Devon's six feet under, but she must believe that he's not the only one capable."

"Who might she have in mind?" I asked, mildly, temporarily setting aside the objection that all the internet chat about the Goddess believing that she had been cursed might be so much hot air. I had to talk around Karen, whose bulk was getting in the way slightly, but Stanley More wasn't overly perturbed by the obstruction.

"The killer, for one. If he was a client from the lunatic fringe, he probably figures that he's got Devon's powers now, if not his talent. I'm not talking about the spirit of Edgar Poe, of course—that one must have its own trajectory, if it really exists. I'm talking about the fundamental magic, if there is any magic…and you have to admit that even if there isn't, things certainly seem to work out as if there were. Are you going to appear in the exhibition, now you've got back together with your first love? Quite a romance, eh?"

"We're not back together," I said. "We don't have any alternative but to co-ordinate our plans, though. We've agreed to be photographed at my place, tomorrow morning. We're hoping that it will end there."

"Fat chance," Kim put in. She was still giving me seemingly-affectionate glances. I wished that her surname wasn't Connor.

I paused for thought for a few seconds, then said: "Do you really think that Curtin was killed by a client from the lunatic fringe?"

"Sure. What Devon believed or didn't believe I can't say, but he was more than willing to pander to people who believed in the magical powers of tattoos. He attracted some who took it very seriously, including whole societies, albeit the sort with not too many members. He wasn't the only one, of course—there's a shop in Southampton that actually uses the name Tattoo Magic, and all tattooists probably have their share of true believers among their clients. Those kinds of people take their dreams seriously, as oracles and shamanistic odysseys....and some, at least, are crazy enough to let themselves be led to drastic action. I always figured that must have been what happened, else the police would soon have found a more commonplace motive when they started digging."

"Did you tell them that when they interviewed you?"

"Sure, but I didn't push the theory too hard, in case they thought I was the crazy one. I was a bit wary about naming any actual suspects, of course—what I knew about it was all second-hand, gleaned from Devon, the group and other members of the fan club. What Armina told them, I don't know. They didn't consider her a suspect, though—that's not why she left the country. Maybe she just went home. She'd been married to an Englishman, but she wasn't English herself. I think she was from the Middle East, although she never actually said so. At any rate, there was nothing much to hold her here once Devon was gone. She was probably harder hit by his death than anyone, including Mel."

I thought about that for a few moments, feeling slightly uneasy. Luscinia's feathers were ruffling again. I couldn't help wondering whether there might be cause to be anxious in the fact that there might be lunatics around who credited her with authentic magical powers of some kind—but I couldn't immediately think of any reason why anyone, however mad, would want to shoot a magical Nightingale...or a bloody Rose.

"Who else?" I asked.

"Who else what?"

"Who else might Armina Holliman, or anyone else, believe to be capable of *lifting the curse*. The killer *for one*, you said. Who else did you have in mind? You? Me? Melanie Millward?"

"Maybe Mel could, if she weren't more interested in making things worse than better. Maybe I could too. I've got some idea of how the trick is worked—in purely psychological terms, of course. I could put on a show of clearing away the evil cobwebs, if I had to. I'm just a gardener, but I'd be willing to bet that I can deploy the power of suggestion as well as the next man, and maybe better than most. Magic or not, suggestion sometimes works, especially on believers. I could probably cure you, Mr. Nightingale, if you were willing to believe in me."

It sounded to me like a big *if*. "What makes you think I'm not well?" I asked him, stonily.

"Your face, for one thing. If I'm reading it right, you haven't been happy for a long time."

"There's a difference between being unhappy and being unwell," I pointed out.

"Is there?" he countered. "Does your Nightingale sing at night, Mr. Ellsworthy? Does it bleed by night? Does it flutter its wings and press harder and harder on to its thorn, in all its masochistic innocence? Are you sure that you're always asleep when it does, or that it actually matters whether you're asleep or awake?"

Obviously, the Tree of the Knowledge of Good and Evil really did bear informative fruit. It had to be guesswork, based on what he'd heard from other "fans", but it was far too accurate for my liking. "Not so much, any more," I muttered, "until all of this came flooding back. Damn Devon Curtin, and the anniversary of his death."

"Damning him isn't what Mel Millward has in mind. Apotheosis, more like. Won't help you, though, will it?"

"Maybe not," I admitted. "But that doesn't help me to believe that you could—or even that I need help at all. I'm not depressed because I'm ill, but because my circumstances are depressing. I'd be crazy if I weren't. As for Lu…the Nightingale, it could be argued that making it the focal point of my bad feelings helps to ease them.

It's the sort of technique a therapist might suggest, to isolate and mask pain."

"Or nurture it and help it grow," More countered. *Touché* again.

He had come off the motorway now on to the A33. There wasn't much traffic around and he reached the town centre in minutes. He obviously knew it reasonably well, because he knew where to find a parking spot, even though the two main streets were heaving with parties of Friday-night drinkers, at least some of whom must have brought designated drivers along to ferry them home.

We walked to the Renaissance. The name that More gave to the desk clerk wasn't Armina Holliman. The room to which we were directed was on the fifth floor. The hotel was quiet, even though it couldn't have been underbooked; I suspected that it would get a good deal noisier when the pubs and clubs began to close.

More even had a special knock: three raps, two and one. After a pause, the door opened slightly, and the tanned face of a woman appeared in the crack. She seemed considerably less well-preserved than Claire or Melanie Millward, although the premature aging of her face was somewhat masked by her expertly-applied make-up. She looked at More fairly carefully, as if making absolutely sure of his identity, but barely glanced at Kim Connor before turning to scan me warily.

I tried to look back, but couldn't. I would never have recognized her as the face in the photographs on the wall of Devon Curtin's studio. Although she couldn't actually be over fifty, she could easily have passed for sixty-five, especially in a harsh light.

"Is this...?" she asked, addressing More, and then winced at her own lack of politeness. "I'm sorry," she said. "I remember you, Kim, but I don't know...."

"The Nightingale," More replied, cutting her off. "I told you I could bring him along, didn't I? He's one of us, although he's only just found out that there is an *us*."

The woman who was presumably Armina Holliman, in spite of appearances, opened the door fully. She was still looking at me. "Come in," she said.

It wasn't until we were inside and she had closed the door that I was able to see and realize the full extent of her deterioration. I knew immediately that it couldn't be due to the mere effects of age. She was ill, and seriously so. She was as thin as a rake, but it was the kind of thinness that even someone like Kim Connor could not have envied. Armina Holliman was frail—perhaps dying.

She offered me a languid hand and said: "I'm glad to meet you, Mr. Ellsworth. I can't say that I've heard a lot about you, but I've long known of your existence. I'm Armina Holliman—formerly The Goddess."

Formerly? I thought, wondering exactly what the word might imply.

I wasn't entirely sure whether I was supposed to shake the hand, kiss it or take it in order to support her while we walked across the room, although I would have hesitated just as much over any of those possibilities. She was wearing a high-necked blouse, a long skirt and woolen tights, so none of her divine attributes was currently on display, but I shuddered at the thought of what they must look like. If The Falling Angel had been stretched to the point of grotesqueness, The Goddess had been diminished to the very brink of mortality.

In the end, I shook the proffered hand gingerly. I would have been very conscious of the poor quality of my clothes if Stanley More and Kim hadn't been every bit as ill-dressed as I was.

The room was plush, but it was just an ordinary hotel room, not a suite. There was only one armchair, and a plastic chair at the desk. I took the plastic chair, and the Goddess insisted that More take the armchair while she and The Falling Angel perched at opposite ends of the bed. It was Kim, in the end, who helped the frail woman to take up that position before moving to her own. It was still me that Armina Holliman was looking at inquisitively, however.

"They've been searching for you too," she said, in a neutral tone.

"They found me," I told her. "I didn't know anything about the exhibition until then. My first impulse was to refuse to be party to it, but it seems that it's not that simple."

"He's found The Rose," More put in. "Or rather, The Rose has found him."

"So now the organizers have located the full set of previously-missing pieces available to them," I commented. "What do *you* have in mind, Ms. Holliman?"

She frowned slightly at the near-rudeness of my informality, but didn't raise any objection—I was, after all, in the company of Stanley More. "I'm not able any longer to take part in such an exhibition, as you can see," she said, slowly. "I'm sure that I can persuade Melanie of that fact easily enough—but I'm reluctant to approach her directly. There was a certain hostility between us twenty years ago. I telephoned Stanley because I thought that he might be prepared to act as an intermediary. When he told me that he'd found you, though...." She paused. "You're probably wondering why I came back at all. I really would like to see the exhibition, if I can. If I thought that I could visit it, incognito...but I don't think that will be possible. I know that I ought to confront Melanie, if only to make her stop searching for me. This must be confusing for you, Mr. Ellsworth, but I can explain...."

She stopped, as if to give the lie to her assurance.

"How have you been, Armina?" Kim asked, as if to fill an awkward silence. Kim could see as well as Stanley or myself how Armina was, but she was fishing for an explanation.

"Not too good, I'm afraid," the other woman replied, attempting a wry smile. "How about you?"

"Not great—as you can doubtless see. Stan's good, though. Stan's always good."

"I survive," said Stanley More, modestly. "Mel's recruiting as many live models as she can. Kim and I are aboard, of course, and at least three others from the old gang. The Masque couldn't do it, though. Health problems. Is that what you mean when you say that you're...unable?"

"It is," Armina Holliman replied, although she seemed slightly ashamed of her own reflexive evasiveness. I could empathize with that. Her gaze flicked back to me again, as if interrogating me about my own stance.

"There's no way that Claire and I are posing live for the exhibition," I said, "in the missionary position or any other. We've agreed to let them take photographs. We're hoping that they'll settle for that."

"I wish you the best of luck," Armina Holliman said. "I'm afraid that my unavailablity might make Melanie all the more enthusiastic to put you on display."

"Is that why you wanted to see me?" I asked. "To apologize?"

She smiled wanly. "Partly," she said. "But not because I might add to Melanie's determination—I'm sure that she'll try with all her might to exploit you to the full in any case. I've read what people are saying on the internet, as you must have done yourself. Gossip appeared to have forged a tentative connection between us, which you might find unfortunate."

"It's all fantasy," I hastened to say.

"Of course it is," she said, "but there's a possibility that *he* might not think so."

"Who?" I got the question in just before Stanley More, who was leaning forward avidly.

"The man who paid for my tattoos and tried to put a curse on Devon Curtin. My former lover, Jacob Marley, also known, to Devon at least, as The Student of Magic."

Jacob Marley, perhaps surprisingly, was a name that had never featured on any of the websites I'd consulted, from which the alias she'd quoted had also been absent. Nor had either name been mentioned by Melanie Millward or Stanley More, The Tree of the Knowledge of Good and Evil. I recognized "Jacob Marley", though, as the name of Scrooge's former partner in *A Christmas Carol*, and the first ghost to come a-haunting him. Inevitably, I suspected that it might be no more authentic than The Student of Magic.

"Is he the one who shot Devon?" This time, Stanley More did get the question in first.

"I really have no idea who shot Devon," Armina Holliman replied, "but I can't believe that it was Marley. It wasn't his style at all. However, I did want to tell The Nightingale the whole story, in case Marley tried to contact him. That's why I asked whether he'd been found when I called you."

It was my prerogative to ask the next question, if anyone were going to, but I didn't have anything specific to ask. I wanted to hear the story of Jacob Marley, who had "tried to put a curse on Devon Curtin". We all did—Kim the Falling Angel no less than Stan the Curiosity-Seeker and me. We waited for her to do that. We weren't exactly sitting comfortably, but she began anyway.

CHAPTER TEN

At first, according to what the former Goddess explained to us, it had been a simple matter of tattooed anklets and wristbands. She had sought those out for herself, not long after her divorce from Malcolm Holliman, a British lawyer specializing in the negotiation of permissions and contracts for the exportation and sale of art and antiques. She had met Holliman in Istanbul. Like many businessmen who traveled a lot, he had an eye for local beauty, although Armina wasn't actually Turkish, having moved to that country from Iran as a child, when the Shah's regime had toppled. Her parents had been thoroughly secularized and Westernized, but were not particularly wealthy—not as wealthy, in fact, as Malcolm Holliman.

Unfortunately, Malcolm Holliman's eye for local beauty had not switched off when he got married. After eight rocky years of wedded unbliss—by which time Armina was twenty-seven—the final collapse had occurred. Although there were no children, Armina had obtained a financial settlement that freed her from need, if not from want. She had been introduced to Jacob Marley several years before as one of her husband's former associates, although it had never been at all clear to her in what role he had played in their business. When he sought a closer relationship in the wake of the divorce, he refused to explain it to her, contenting himself with saying that he had been responsible for handling the trickier aspects of the trade, and that he did not want to dwell on a relationship with her former husband that he had now severed.

The designs for the anklet and bracelet tattoos had been selected from Devon Curtin's catalogue of flash. Armina had been pleased with him, but Marley had apparently been even more delighted with the artist's work, and had encouraged her to proceed with further ornamentation, eventually funding the work and taking over the planning of the decorations, which Curtin had executed according to his designs. Marley had also become a client of Curtin's himself, although he had asked the tattooist to keep their relationship strictly confidential, perhaps because of some slight embarrassment about the nature of the tattoos he wanted for himself, which were also of his own design.

According to Armina, only three people ever saw the designs inscribed in Marley's flesh: her, Curtin and Marley himself. No photographs were taken, so the work required no title, but Curtin had improvised one anyway, for use in private conversation. Marley was nowhere near as well-to-do as Malcolm Holliman had been, but he had ambition. Armina's bodily decoration was, in part, an expression of that ambition—but also, if his claims were to be taken seriously, partly a means to its furtherance. She was supposed to be more than a mere symbol of the wealth to come; like a voodoo doll intended for benign rather than malign purposes, she was a kind of fetish whose adornment was supposed to help bring about a real increase in wealth for her designer. Marley's own secret decorations were magical symbols intended to have a similar effect: that of enhancing his own powers as a magician.

Armina was never completely sure whether Marley believed in his own impostures, but she was quite certain that Devon Curtin did not—even though Curtin spared no effort in encouraging his client's apparent beliefs, presumably for mercenary reasons. Armina, meanwhile, became increasingly enthusiastic about her own gradual transformation. She was flattered by the attention lavished on her by both men. She wanted to be a work of art, and knew that mere nudes were ten a penny in the world of art. The idea of transforming her own nudity into something artificially decorative appealed to her very strongly.

I didn't have to theorize for myself about the nature of Armina's eventual infatuation with Devon Curtin. She likened it herself to the kind of "transference" that is sometimes said to occur between psychotherapists and their patients, and to the well-known mutual magnetism that often brings artists and their models together. Indeed, she went further than that.

"Psychologists know," she said, "that stimulation of the nervous system is psychologically negotiable—open to interpretation. It's by no means uncommon for people to 'translate' potentially-unpleasant intense sensations into potentially-pleasant ones, especially erotic attraction. Females who submit to the tattooist's needle have the psychological option of transforming at least a fraction of their pain into lust—although I can assure you, based on experience, that it doesn't work nearly as well if the tattooist is also female. Devon asked Melanie to finish off one of my designs, while she was ambitious to become his apprentice, because the work was easier to execute left-handed than right-handed. It didn't work out well—not in the technical sense, but in terms of our attitude to one another. She might have got a very different response from a male client—and probably did so routinely, when she took over the studio. At any rate, it seemed to intensify her hostility when she became aware that Devon had slept with me, although straightforward jealousy was presumably the primary instigator."

It wasn't hard to see how that might work. I wondered whether it might have been Melanie who had tipped Marley off that his voodoo doll was being compromised. Armina didn't offer any speculations of that sort, though. She continued with her own story, which was becoming fairly predictable. She and Curtin had a fling, more at her instigation than his. Curtin certainly hadn't been in love with her, and had, in fact, begun to treat her with amused contempt when she became infatuated with him. It was then that he had begun to refer to her as "Lydia", much to her annoyance.

One way or another, Marley had found out about the affair, and had become extremely annoyed himself, apparently more because of the potential effect on Armina's supposed magical utility than the sexual infidelity *per se*. If Melanie *had* tipped him off, it was presumably in the hope that Marley would ditch his puppet, but that hadn't been the result. It had been Curtin, not Armina, at whom Marley had directed his wrath. He had, in fact, seemed intent on "saving" Armina, not so much from imagined sexual depredations, but from magical spoliation. Marley wanted to recover her value as a talisman, a promise of future success.

Given that, I could understand why Armina reckoned that it wasn't Marley's style to go after Curtin with a gun, or even with his fists. In order to achieve his delusory end, Marley had to go after Curtin with magic—and that was what he had tried to do. When the time next came to settle his account he wrote a curse on the back of the check.

"What was the curse, exactly?" Stanley More interrupted, when Armina reached that part in her story.

"If I remember correctly," she said, "the exact wording was: *May all the troubles of this world descend upon you, and may the anticipation of your allotted place in Hell echo in your living soul.* The implication of writing it on the back of a check was, I suppose, that by depositing the check, Devon would somehow be accepting the curse, bringing it down upon himself. However skeptical Devon might have been, I think he hesitated over that. I don't know for sure whether he deposited the check or not, but I suspect not. At any rate, there was a quarrel between them—which, as you can imagine, became heated. Devon blamed me for the whole thing. So did Melanie Millward. I blamed Marley—but I wouldn't have left him, if other circumstances hadn't developed. The pity of it all is that Marley's magical work would have been undone regardless. Fate intervened—although I wasn't at all sure then, and still harbor slight nagging doubts, that the intervention was due to mere chance rather than something more sinister. Marley would certainly have thought so, and I'd been with him long enough to have been infected by his superstition."

"What happened?" Kim Connor was agog to know.

"I was diagnosed with breast cancer. It was already sufficiently advanced for the consultant to recommend an immediate double mastectomy. That was only the beginning, of course. I needed a course of chemotherapy. I began it in London, on the day that Devon was shot, but when my parents got the news they wanted me to go to Germany, where one of my cousins was involved in a clinical trial of a new chemotherapeutic regime that seemed promising. My consultant agreed that it might improve my chances, so I flew to Munich as soon as the police had finished questioning me about

Devon's death. I wasn't a suspect, because I'd been in a bed at Guy's with a drip in my arm at the time of the shooting."

"But Marley must have been a suspect," I said. My eyes, I knew, were now fixed on her bosom. The breasts outlined by her blouse had to be fake, but they were adequate to deceive the unwary eye, which couldn't possibly tell that the tattooed brassière was no longer there, any more than the flesh on which it had been imprinted.

"Presumably. Perhaps he had an alibi too. I don't know—I never saw him again. I never saw anyone again. I never told anyone outside of my family about the cancer, the surgery or the chemotherapy. At that time, I thought of it as something shameful, something that needed to be kept secret from everyone except my parents. I didn't want anyone who had known me as The Goddess to know what had become of the work of art—but I would have been equally secretive, I suppose, had I never been given any such title, or burdened with any expectations and delusions of grandeur at all."

I understood then why Armina had been so anxious when she discovered that Melanie Millward was looking for her, in order to put her on exhibition, and why she felt that approaching Melanie was such a delicate matter that she needed a go-between. I understood, too, why she might have thought that Stanley More might not be the ideal ambassador, even though he was the only person she could easily contact. Kim the Falling Angel didn't seem to me to be any more promising. Once again, I realized that, by comparison with the fates of Devon Curtin's other works of art, I might be reckoned to have got off easily. If The Student of Magic really had accumulated sufficient knowledge and authority to make his curse effective, it certainly hadn't limited itself to Curtin's own person. But where did I fit in? Obviously, in rational terms, I didn't—but where did the lunatic fringe think that I fitted in, given that its members didn't seem to know about Armina's cancer?

I didn't have to raise the question explicitly. Armina was already progressing to that.

"I knew that Devon had been thinking about doing a double design based on Oscar Wilde's story about the Nightingale and the Rose for some while," she said. "I'd mentioned it to Marley. He had already become suspicious of Devon by that time—not just about the possibility that he might be sleeping with me, but about the possibility that Devon might have magical ambitions of his own. That was nonsensical, as I knew perfectly well—but Marley didn't. He thought that Devon was fooling me in more ways than one. I knew that he'd begun to worry about the possible relevance of the Nightingale and the Rose to his own project, because of the coincidence of Devon referring to him as a Student and his own plan to deck my naked flesh with magical diamonds—but I didn't know, before I left the country, that Devon had actually completed such a design. The police never mentioned it when they questioned me, and I had no further contact with Melanie or Marley. It seems that Marley wasn't the only person to have made the connection, though. At the moment, as you said yourself, Mr. Ellsworth, it's just a fantasy, and one among many…but there are still three months to go before the exhibition opens. Melanie seems to be hungry for whatever publicity she can get, in which case…."

In which case, I thought, it was a pity that Armina had just told the whole story to Stan the Tree of Knowledge, who was obviously not a man to keep his fruits to himself, or to Kim the Fallen Angel, whose bloated head with its child-like face did not give the appearance of being safe custody for secrets. On the other hand, once Melanie had found Armina, and had obtained an explanation of why she couldn't provide an exhibit, the game would have been up anyway. Melanie would then have felt free to use any story she could find for publicity purposes, whether or not it had the slightest grounding in fact or supposition. Armina's desire to warn me that there might be at least one man with a serious interest in the possibility of a magical connection between The Nightingale and The Goddess had been motivated by mere altruism…and it really was something I was glad to know.

What I really wanted and needed to know, of course, was how "Jacob Marley" might react to the news that I had been identified and found at last. That was my next question.

"I don't know," she replied, unhelpfully. "Devon could probably have made a much better guess than I can. Marley might think that whatever Devon had been trying to do—not, of course, that he was actually trying to do anything, except create a work of art—had been aborted by his death. On the other hand…well, I suppose a good deal hangs on how he's fared these last twenty years. If he's grown rich, he'll probably be well content with his magic. If he hasn't, and feels that his magical attempts to make his fortune were somehow thwarted, he might be enthusiastic to take action of some sort. If he thinks that Devon's creation of The Nightingale and the Rose somehow broke or perverted his own spell, he might be eager to repair the breach, even after twenty years."

Which brought us to the ultimate question. "Am I in danger, Ms. Holliman?" I asked, bluntly. "Is *Claire* in danger?"

"I simply don't know," was the inevitable reply. "But knowing Marley as I did, I can't give you a cast-iron guarantee that you aren't."

That should have been the punch-line to the story—and would have been had I been there on my own, but I wasn't. Stanley More was there too, and he had his own agenda. "Do you still have bad dreams, Armina?" he asked.

"Of course I still have bad dreams," she said. "In the last nineteen years I've had three bouts of cancer, fearful every day between bouts that it might return at any moment. It was almost a relief when it came back for a third bite, and I knew that there was no longer any hope of getting away from it."

"Isn't there?" Kim put in, her voice full of sympathy and pity.

"None at all," Armina said. "I've had all the chemotherapy I can take. If I'm lucky, I might have six months to live. If I'm unlucky…well, I could drop dead tomorrow. Not that I'm entirely sure that I've got that the right way around." She meant that dropping dead might be the more fortunate eventuality.

"Are you willing to tell Mr. Ellsworth about the dreams?" More persisted. He was using me; it was his own curiosity he wanted fed.

"Why not? It's not the cancer dreams that interest you, of course—it's the ones I had before; the ones I had while Devon was turning me into The Goddess. I never told Marley the detail of them, any more than I spelled them out to you and your ghoulish little group, although I was less shy about reporting them to Devon. I didn't think of them as nightmares, in the very beginning, and certainly not as revelations. In fact, at first I thought of them as ordinary erotic dreams, of the sort that any woman might have who has been used to a steady diet of marital sex and then finds herself alone. The fact that the jewelry was increasingly integrated into the dreams after I began a sexual relationship with Marley and began to elaborate my bodily ornamentation further didn't seem in the least unusual. In the dreams, of course, the jewels were solid, not mere sketches in subcutaneous ink. They were heavy—and they were powerful. They were a lure, and they were an essential part of the erotic play that the dreams involved. It was as if they were artificial erogenous zones. I'm not going to go into detail, but the sex I had…dreamed that I had…while wearing them wasn't at all orthodox—which didn't make it any less exciting, as you can probably imagine.

"In spite of their increasing frequency and intensity, I continued to think of them as ordinary erotic dreams for quite some time, although I did wonder whether I might somehow be becoming addicted to them. At first, after the divorce, I'd felt too numb and depressed to feel much urgency about finding an actual sexual outlet, although I was young enough and beautiful enough to attract would-be-seducers in quantity. When I took up with Marley, it wasn't lust that drove me; I was simply surrendering to what seemed to be inevitability. When the dreams became more insistent instead of less, almost as if they were striving to take over that part of my being, I felt even less inclined physically—but I let Marley do what he wanted with me. I didn't even go after Devon merely because I was besotted with him, in spite of the transfiguration wrought by his needlework. I would have been perfectly capable of accommodating him within my dreams—but somehow, that didn't seem honest.

"Sleeping with Devon didn't stem the flow of the dreams, but it did alter them. They became darker, and more confused. Again, I'm not going to go into detail, but your imagination can probably fill in the blanks with sufficient accuracy. The partners that my own imagination conjured up became more sinister, actively cruel…although it didn't diminish the intensity of the experience at all.

"In the beginning, it hadn't even occurred to me to wonder whether the partners I imagined were anything more than figments of my imagination—mere masturbatory props. The idea that there might somehow be *someone else* in my dreams would have seemed utterly ludicrous, even though I knew that Marley fancied himself a magician. When the idea did occur to me, it seemed too far-fetched to be remotely plausible…but as the dreams became increasingly intense and peculiar, though, the suspicion came to seem gradually less absurd, and proportionately ominous. Along with it came a host of corollary suspicions—including the suspicion that the person using my dream-self as a courtesan goddess might be aware that someone else was using my actual body in a not-entirely-dissimilar fashion…profaning his jewels, as it were.

"That was why I felt obliged to investigate Devon's other clients, in order to find out whether they too had dreams, and of what sort. You were easy to find, Mr. More. You introduced me to Kim and the others, so that we could all compare notes. That was more than a little absurd too, I suppose—five or six of us meeting up in a pub in Holborn, huddled in a corner booth, coyly swapping dreams, but always offering sly hints rather than specifics, trying all the while to analyze them, like psychotherapists or shamanic healers."

Stanley More nodded in agreement, glancing at me to confirm that what Armina was saying was true—even the bit about it all being more than a little absurd.

"We all had dreams," Armina continued, now looking directly at me, while I concentrated on meeting her gaze like any normal person, "but the most absurd thing of all, in all probability, was that we couldn't be sure that there was anything sinister, or even significant, about the fact. What could be more natural, in fact, than the fact that we built the imagery of our body art into our private fantasies? All of the others were self-made individuals, even if they'd taken suggestions and guidance from Devon as to what images to have imprinted where. If any of the other members of the group were believers in magic, they never identified themselves as such. We all posed as conductors of a serious scientific investigation, gathering evidence and suggesting hypotheses."

Stanley More was still nodding, lending his endorsement to the narrative. Kim Connor was listening intently, and didn't seem to be in the least bored. She was as curious about the dreams as Stanley was—perhaps unsurprisingly, if they had continued to meet to discuss them on a regular basis or twenty years.

"We never invited Devon to join in, nor Melanie," Armina continued, still addressing me. "That probably seems silly to you, Mr. Ellsworth, as they were the two people likely to be able to give us the information we needed to move forward, but we were all in awe of Devon, and a little afraid of him—not because we thought he might laugh at us, but because we really were beginning to suspect that we might have been the victims of magic…of a spell, or a curse. We weren't afraid of Melanie, of course, except in the sense that we knew that anything we said to her would be passed on to Devon, but I didn't like her and she didn't like me. There was a measurable tension. She never referred to me as 'The Goddess', always as 'Lydia'—and she referred to our little circle as 'the groupies'.

"Maybe it was all a matter of collective folly. Maybe we talked ourselves into it, when an objective voice could have deflated the entire balloon, but we…I, at least…really did begin to suspect that there was something supernatural in what had been done to us, and what was still happening to us. Even if it was all a mere matter of suggestion, we thought there was a strong possibility that the suggestion had been deliberately planted, that our dreams were being deliberately steered and supplied. Then Devon was shot, and the balloon *was* pricked. I don't know what the others said when they were interviewed by the police, but I didn't mention dreams, spells, curses or suggestion at all.

"On the other hand, the dreams didn't stop. They never have. The jewels still figure large within them—I assume that's what you want to know, Mr. More—and in much the same fashion as they always did: the apparatus of lust and torment. Over time, however, they've become confused with my image of my cancer. My doctors actually advised that: to visualize the cancer cells in some fashion, so that I could imagine myself fighting them, thus mobilizing my inner resources. For all I know, it worked: at any rate, that first course of experimental chemotherapy was successful. I was clear for seven years. The dreams never went away, though. The jewelry was still there, within my flesh, even though the harmony of the art-work had been scarred and spoiled. The war never ended; it just became dormant…and it flared up again in due course. And then, after another period of relative quiescence, it began again. I've never entirely escaped from the grip of the cancerous gems…the curse of the cancerous gems, if that's the way you want to look at it. But if I am cursed, who cursed me? Was it Devon? Was it Marley? In either case, why? I can't help wondering, even though I know that it's stupid. I'll tell you one thing, though, Mr. More, and that's that if the only thing you're cursed with is knowledge, you're a damn sight luckier than I am."

"True," Stanley More conceded, although the way he said it suggested that he was still guarding dark secrets of his own. "And if Kim's dreams were limited to expressions of her weight problems, that would be trivial too. But Mr. Ellsworth, at least, has had a harder time, if I'm not mistaken."

"I can't compare my misfortunes with Ms. Holliman's," I said defensively. "Any pain I've felt has been largely self-inflicted. I know that."

"Has it, though?" Stanley More murmured. "Has it?"

"Do you dream about The Nightingale?" Kim asked, with a sympathetic softness in her voice. "I dream about The Angel…I know all about his agony…but he really did bring it on himself, for selfish reasons. The Nightingale is dying on behalf of someone else…The Student."

It wasn't obvious that she'd actually read the story. I suspected that she might have got a garbled version from Stanley. "Actually," I said, keeping my own voice soft and trying to sound sympathetic, "it was on behalf of Love that the Nightingale made her sacrifice. The Student conned her—perhaps unwittingly—and her sacrifice proved to be in vain. The Nightingale was the Student's fool."

"And how did she feel about that, Mr. Ellsworth?" Stanley More put in, mimicking a therapist. He didn't have to elaborate, either for my benefit or Armina Holliman's.

"Bitter," I said. "Resentful. Hurt." I knew that I didn't have to explain how I knew.

"You've been disappointed in love yourself, Cris, haven't you?" Kim asked, with exaggerated softness—as if she wanted to comfort and compensate me.

"More than once," I said, seeing no need to be coy about it. "Claire—The Rose—and I broke up before the scabs had fallen away from the tattoos. Like you, Ms. Holliman, I'm divorced—and my relationship with my daughter was fractured in the process, although we never lost contact. I never imagined that any of it might be the effects of a curse, though. Why should it be? Things like that happen all the time, routinely. Even cancer is commonplace, an evil sufficient in itself not to require the assistance of human malevolence. Who had any motive to curse me...us? What could anyone possibly hope to gain?"

"But you *are* saying that the nightingale reflects your own pain, Cris," Kim continued, relentless in spite of the affectionate softness of her tone. "In your dreams, at least."

"In dreams that won't stay confined to sleep?" Stanley More added. It was Armina's turn to listen now, and she seemed to be taking as keen an interest as I had in her story.

"Yes," I admitted, in response to both rhetorical questions. "Although...sometimes, it feels more as if the nightingale *is* my pain...an embodiment of it rather than a mere reflection. When she sings, and bleeds, in my dreams...." I left it at that. Armina hadn't spelled out the filthy detail of her orgasmic fantasies; why should I spell out the stupid ignominies of mine?

"What about the Rose?" Kim continued.

"Until I met her today in Starbuck's, I hadn't seen her in the best part of twenty years," I said. "We did a little bit of catching up, but she wasn't ready to tell me her address, let alone the intimate secrets of her dreams. She does have dreams, though, and bad ones—she told me that much, and implied that they reflected...or embodied...her own troubles. She's on her own now too; she didn't tell me anything about her ex-husband but she had a son who died of leukemia. The details don't matter. We can take it for granted that she's in the same boat as the rest of us, dreamwise. So what?"

"You've seen what people are saying," Kim went on. "That the work can only be seen as it was intended to be seen if the two of you actually make love." It finally dawned on me that she, at least, was still hoping for some magical redemption—that the completion of Devon Curtin's final work of art of magic might somehow put things right. The fantasists who wrote cryptic notes on the web about the possibility of The Nightingale lifting the curse on The Goddess were actually talking about the possibility of lifting what they considered to be their own curses. I suddenly understood Stanley More's motivation a little more clearly—and also his extreme reluctance to spell it out explicitly.

"I've read the rumors," I admitted. "I've also concluded, with a little help from Melanie Millward, that the work never can or will be seen as Curtin might have intended, given that she and I aren't twenty any more. We lost our chance…there won't ever be another."

That seemed to put a spoke in Kim's wheel. She became silent, pensive and disappointed.

"That's only true," Armina Holliman pointed out, after a pause, "if you think about the work purely and simply as a matter of visual art. You can't reproduce now what Devon saw in *you*, with an artist's eye for an interesting pair of models, but.…" She didn't have to finish the sentence.

"But from a magical point of view," I finished, for her, "it might be a different matter. Except that Claire and I aren't about to get involved in that kind of performance for anyone's profit or pleasure."

"Not even your own?" Armina enquired. The question would have seemed insolent if Stanley More had voiced it, but it didn't seem unduly intrusive, coming from The Goddess, whose private parts could be seen in brazen photographic display at various intersections in the World Wide Web.

"We fell out of love a long time ago," I said. "I doubt that we can fall back into it, even if we are both unattached and troubled." The romantic twinge reasserted itself, though. There are dreams and dreams—and we all experience both kinds, always being suckers for the logic of story-telling, the esthetic rewards of happy endings. I could almost hear Karen saying: "Go for it, Dad. What have you got to lose?"

The ex-Goddess didn't press the point. She became pensive.

"Would you like to see the others, Armina?" More asked her. "I'm still in contact with most of them."

"Not just now," she replied. "I dare say that we'll all meet up before the exhibition, if we can…soon, given that I'm on a tight schedule...but not just now. I have to see Melanie first. That won't be easy."

"What about Marley?" Stanley More put in. "Are you going to see him?"

"I have no idea where he is—and no one seems to be looking for him, as they were for Mr. Ellsworth. So far as I can tell, there are no photographs of his secret tattoos, and no mention of his ironic title, anywhere in cyberspace."

"Maybe no one's looking for him," I said, "but that doesn't mean that he's not looking for you...or for us."

"I'm not in the least afraid of him," Armina Holliman stated, flatly. "If I have the chance to meet him again...well, it won't quite be akin to your meeting with The Rose, but hopefully not too different. It's just a matter of getting used to the idea. I'll be sure to let you know if he does get in touch."

"Thanks," I said. "Would you like me to talk to Melanie on your behalf? I'll probably see her tomorrow, after the photo-shoot if not during. I can arrange a meeting without letting her know where you're staying, if that's what you want."

Stanley More frowned, as if I were usurping his privilege, but he straightened his face almost immediately; he didn't want Armina to be disappointed in him.

Armina thought about the proposition carefully, and eventually said: "Yes, I think I would—but please don't rush into it. Wait for a moment of calm before you try to explain the situation to her. Then, if you wouldn't mind reporting her reaction back to me be-fore...well, we'll plan the next step then. You're very kind. So are you, Stanley—I don't know what I'd have done if I hadn't been able to call you. I feel a little better now. It was nice to see you again too, Kim."

It was an obvious sign of dismissal—she suddenly seemed very tired, as was only to be expected.

The three of us rose slowly to our feet, while Armina rearranged herself into a more comfortable position on the bed. "I'm sure we'll all meet up again," she said. "We have things in common, after all."

Dutifully, we showed ourselves out, bidding her goodnight as we went.

"The jigsaw is coming together," Stanley More remarked, as we went down in the lift.

"It appears so," I conceded. "Let's hope it makes a pretty picture when it's done."

CHAPTER ELEVEN

That night, unsurprisingly, I had bad dreams. The dreams featured a blood-stained rose as well as nightingales. They also featured needles, of several different sorts—merciful acupuncture needles as well as viciously pricking kinds—and mysterious figures in hooded jackets armed with guns and knives. There were chases, and intervals in which I was weighed down, unable to flee, while my heart fluttered within my breast like a trapped bird.

There were quieter intervals, too—erotic intervals in which I saw myself, as if from a distance, making love to a woman swathed in jewelry—not tattoos representing jewelry, but actual jewelry, comprising precious stones by the score mounted in gold and silver. She sang, but it was a nightingale's song, replete with plaintive anguish—and blood dripped from her eyes, which had been punctured in order to blind her to the splendors of her own gleaming body.

I eventually woke up feeling exhausted, although I knew that I had slept for a long time. It was past the hour at which I usually woke—eight rather than seven—and I hastened through my shower, thanking the Lord that Claire had been as good as her word the previous afternoon, and had helped me to put the house, especially the spare bedroom, into a fit condition to receive a visitor armed with a camera. I had stripped the single bed of its sheet and duvet, and wrapped the mattress in an old coverlet, so that it looked more like a couch than a place where anyone might actually sleep.

The room had been Karen's when she had been a small child, although she now used the larger spare room when she came to stay. There was more room in that one to store and display a collection of personal belongings that had accumulated steadily over the years, in the interests of making the house a home from home.

Claire's Datsun pulled up in the driveway at five to ten. A red Citroen followed less than twenty minutes later, similarly before the appointed time. Claire and I both watched from the sitting room window as Melanie Millward got out of the second vehicle, pausing to unload various items of equipment before advancing to the door.

"How could she resist the temptation?" I muttered. "She must have had plenty of practice taking pictures of tattoos, after Curtin's death if not before. She was never going to entrust this job to anyone else if she could help it."

When I opened the door and reintroduced Melanie to Claire, she asked me if I'd help her bring the equipment in, so I walked back with her to the pile she'd built up beside the rear passenger door.

"Thank you for agreeing to this," she said. "It will fill an awkward gap in the story told by the exhibition—not quite the climax, but a significant part of its final phase." For the moment, she wasn't trying to push for anything further.

She made a slight grimace when I took her upstairs to inspect the spare bedroom, but approved it anyway, presumably having taken note of the rest of the house and reasoning that there would be nowhere better. I couldn't be of much help setting up the lights and the digital camera—which seemed absurdly small perched on a long-legged tripod—so I just stood and watched. Claire stood very close to me, as if huddling for protection.

I took off my shirt first. Claire hesitated, but eventually gritted her teeth and stripped to the waist. Her breasts were larger than I remembered, but less firm. When she lay down on her back, though, with her left side toward the lens, they formed a pleasantly rounded curve.

I hadn't seen the rose in a long time. It seemed smaller than I had remembered, and not as bright—but when I had seen it last, the skin had still been somewhat inflamed, and the scabs had not entirely peeled away. Once I had positioned myself, though—very gingerly, in the hope of avoiding any offensive contact—I couldn't see the whole piece. Only Melanie could do that.

I had to fight to control the flow of my hormones—more adrenalin than testosterone—but the ex-receptionist didn't seem at all stressed, let alone entranced. She was very businesslike. "I need you to come a little further forward, Cris," she said. "It's a matter of lining up the blood drops. A little further…that's perfect. Hold that pose." At least she didn't say "Watch the birdie."

I did as I was told, following all her orders as best I could, striving all the while to simulate dispassion.

If Claire and I had hoped that it would all be over in a trice, we would have been direly disappointed. Melanie wanted us closer together, and then still closer. She wanted our outstretched arms to be just right. The positions weren't easy to hold—especially mine, which required delicate balancing on one elbow. The elbow in question soon began to ache, and then to suffer stabbing pains. Luscinia was silent, though; I couldn't feel a thing in my side, or in my heart.

Melanie moved the camera three times, altering the angle in subtle ways. She took her time. We had a break half way through, but from beginning to end the shoot took three quarters of an hour.

Then we had a cup of tea. At least, Melanie and I did. Claire had strong black coffee, which she sipped greedily, as if she were in dire need of the caffeine boost, although she was obviously relieved to have her bra and blouse back on again.

"Two down," Melanie said. "Only one to go, and we can reckon the exhibition reasonably complete."

I was tempted to explain to her there and then that she could set aside her hopes on that score, but I hesitated. It would have been a cheap piece of one-upmanship to gloat about having found The Goddess, as I'd found The Rose, before her, and I wasn't sure that we'd yet reached the "moment of calm" that Armina had specified. I was still wound up, and Claire seemed to be drowning in embarrassment. In any case, I wanted to do a little more fishing myself before I told Melanie about the previous evening's adventure. Tentatively, I said: "Did you know that you were followed here yesterday by the Tree of the Knowledge of Good and Evil?"

Her surprise was momentary, and she didn't seem overly annoyed. "You mustn't mind Stan," she said. "He's been buzzing around like an avid bluebottle all week, but he's harmless. He'll be gathering his little cabal together, I don't doubt: Steve the King of Hearts, Kim the Falling Angel and Howard the Serpent Prince. Did he tell you about the curse?"

"He mentioned something of the sort," I said, cautiously. "He thinks that other people might come looking for us—Claire and me, that is. People who think that we can lift the curse."

Claire's face clouded over when I said that, but she was content to cradle her black coffee in her hands, sipping from the cup at regular intervals

"What curse?" Melanie said, contemptuously. "You know as well as I do, Cris, that there never was any curse. Not that I'm ungrateful for the speculation, mind—we can make capital out of it, if we play our cards right. Stan's a valuable man to have around, in that sense, although I've never been able to figure out whether he's primarily interested in lifting the curse or identifying the murderer. Either way, he wants to be the man who solved the mystery."

"It would be good publicity for the exhibition if he did solve the murder mystery," I pointed out. "That would be quite a coup, wouldn't it?—if your retrospective helped to flush Curtin's murderer out, after all these years."

"Yes it would," she agreed. "We can but hope—but I wouldn't put my money on Stan More being the man to do it. That Tree went to his head as soon as I finished it off. He thinks he knows it all, but he's an idiot really."

"You finished it off?" I said.

"Sure. Devon often got me to help him out on a lot of his major pieces—not because he was consciously training me up, but because I'm left-handed. That makes it more difficult for me to write—script is designed to be written left-to-right, so that the writing hand is always ahead of the pen's flow—but visual representation is a different matter, especially when the contours of the human body have to be taken into account. Some designs are easier to execute if the needle moves right-to-left, and there are likely to be parts of any large complex design that are better-wrought left-handed. It gives me an edge over the competition. I've long since overcome the slight awkwardness of inscribing MOTHER or JULIE on the arms of butch blokes who want to show off their sentimental side, but right-handed needlers never bother to practice mirror-writing. It gives me a different perspective—and that's invaluable, if you're ambitious to do real art-work."

I had never seen her so enthusiastic; for once, she'd allowed herself to get carried away. If I'd been interested in what she was saying, I'd have encouraged her to continue in that vein—but I had an agenda of my own.

"Do you think Devon's murderer might be one of your living models?" I asked. "Or will he—or she—only come along to the exhibition as a member of the audience, to gloat about remaining undiscovered for such a long time?"

Melanie frowned, perhaps because she'd been so rudely interrupted in the flow of her own enthusiasm, but perhaps because she simply didn't like that line of questioning. She opened her mouth, but I doubted that she was actually going to answer the question. At any rate, she was saved by the ringing doorbell.

As it was Saturday, I hoped that it might be Karen, while half-expecting that it was Stanley More, doggedly playing the role of bad penny. In order to find out, I went to the window and peered out. I couldn't see inside the porch, but I could see the police car parked behind the red Citroen.

"It's the police," I said, faintly astonished.

"Oh shit!" said Melanie. "Can't they stop harassing me about that bloody check?"

"What check?" I asked, as I crossed the sitting room.

"Nothing important," Melanie muttered. "Just some piece of twenty-year-old evidence they couldn't find again after they'd opened the files. They think one of us nicked it while we were checking the notebook—absurd!"

I would have liked to find out more, but I had to get to the front door. When I opened it, I was confronted by two women in uniform. One of them was only a Community Support Officer, but the other was a real policewoman. They wore the kind of serious expression that the police always adopt when they want to emphasize the gravity of a situation.

"Is it Karen?" was the first thing I said, fearfully, before they'd even told me their names.

"Crispin Ellsworthy?" said the policewoman, who had named herself as W.P.C. Craig while I had been voicing my anxious question.

"Yes," I said. "Has something happened to my daughter?"

"This doesn't concern your daughter, sir. We'd like you to come to the station to answer a few questions, if that's all right." Her tone implied that it had better be all right, unless I had an exceedingly good excuse.

"Are you arresting me?" I asked.

"No sir. It's just that we think that you might be able to help us with an enquiry into an incident that took place in the early hours of this morning."

"I was at home, in bed," I said, conscious that it wasn't much of an alibi. I was also conscious that Claire and Melanie were now pressing close behind me, hidden from the gaze of the W.P.C. by the half-open door, but eager to catch every word.

"No one's disputing that, sir," the policewoman said. "It's just that you might have some information relevant to our enquiry."

"What incident, exactly?" I asked.

"The details are confidential, I'm afraid, sir. We can't discuss it here. C.I.D. will probably fill you in, when they talk to you. Will you come with us, sir?"

I looked around at my two temporary guests, neither of whom was in any hurry to say that they would leave the house immediately and let me get on with it. Quite the contrary, in fact—they both gave the impression of wanting to stay, in order to await my return. They wanted to know what this was about just as much as I did.

"All right," I said to the policewoman. "I'll just get my jacket." As Claire and Melanie stepped back to let me pass, I said: "Don't feel compelled to wait for me. I might be gone for some time, as Captain Oates said."

The both assured me that they didn't mind. There was a glint in Melanie's eye, which suggested that the prospect of an opportunity to exercise her persuasive arts on Claire was by no means unwelcome. Claire didn't seem unduly intimidated by that prospect, however—which was perhaps as well, since her car was trapped by

Melanie's and couldn't get out of the driveway unless Melanie moved the red Citroen first.

The police car got me to the station within five minutes, without having to use its siren. There was no hanging around; I was ushered in to an interview room with two plain clothes officers almost immediately. They explained that they would be taking a statement on behalf of their colleagues at Reading Station, trying to imply by means of their tone of voice that Thames Valley Police was one big happy family.

The two detectives asked me whether I had accompanied a man named Stanley More to Reading on the previous evening. I admitted that I had, and then confirmed that Kim Connor had also accompanied us. The detectives checked the time of our arrival and departure. They already knew that we'd been to the Renaissance Hotel to meet a woman whose real name was Armina Holliman, although she had registered under an alias. They wanted to know the details of our conversation.

I'd been through the whole routine before, twenty years ago. My account was as elaborately detailed this time as it had been then. I didn't leave anything out or dress anything up. Only when I'd finished did I say: "Has something happened to Ms. Holliman?"

"I'm afraid so," said the senior detective, one D.S. Williamson.

"Is she dead?"

"I'm afraid so."

"But she didn't just die of cancer, I presume?"

"The circumstances are...unclear."

"Suspicious, you mean?"

"It's too early to speculate," D.S. Williamson assured me—which I took to be an affirmative answer in disguise.

"But you think there's a link to the murder of Devon Curtin?" I persisted. "You think that the person who killed him might also have killed her?"

That was too luscious for the detective to resist. "What makes you think that, Mr. Ellsworth?" he said, attempting blandness but failing.

"Were you listening, just now?" I said. "I've just told you that we discussed the murder, and the possibility that the whole thing might get stirred up again. Was this Jacob Marley character interviewed twenty years ago?"

"I'm not at liberty to discuss that," D.S. Williamson informed me, dully. "Do you have any further information pertaining to that inquiry, or this one?"

I hesitated. I wondered whether my description of the previous night's conversation about tattoo magic and curses has irredeemably undermined my apparent reliability as a witness, and whether, if it hadn't, there was anything more I could say that wouldn't complete the job.

"Jacob Marley is a character in *A Christmas Carol*," I said. "It's probably an alias—but if he was one of Curtin's clients, his real name might appear in his accounts, and Melanie Millward might be able to pick it out. You can probably make as good a guess as I can as to what the trickier aspects of Malcolm Holliman's arts and antiques business might have been." I figured that, being policemen, they would immediately have formed the hypothesis that there might have been drug-smuggling involved, especially as that had been the speculative motive of choice for Devon's murder.

Then something clicked, and another thought suddenly struck me. "The check that went missing from the evidence file," I said, "wouldn't, by any chance, be the check with Marley's curse written on it?"

"How do you know about that?" D.S. Williamson was quick to ask.

I was about to remind him that I'd just told him what Armina had told me when I realized that what he meant was how I knew that a check had gone missing from the evidence file. "Melanie mentioned that you'd been harassing her about it," I said, not choosing my words as carefully as I might have done.

"Do you know where Ms. Millward is now?" the detective asked.

"Not for certain, but I suspect that she's still at my house. She spent the morning taking photographs for her exhibition...of The Nightingale and the Rose...and she was still there when the W.P.C. came to pick me up. She might have gone by now, though. I suppose

I should have told her about seeing Armina but....well, it doesn't matter now."

I couldn't help wondering, though, whether Melanie would be sorry or delighted to hear that Armina Holliman was dead. Given that The Goddess was unfit for exhibition, the publicity generated by her sudden death could only benefit the exhibition—rather more so than her death from cancer would have done, if it did turn out that the cancer hadn't been the cause. I had to remind myself that I still had no idea what might have happened.

Once I'd told D.S. Williamson that Melanie might still be at my house, he became noticeably more enthusiastic to have me driven back there immediately, although he warned me, dutifully, that he might have more questions to ask me later.

CHAPTER TWELVE

It turned out that Melanie was still at the house when W.P.C. Craig drove me back, and was distinctly annoyed when she was whisked away to the station without being given a chance to quiz me on what had happened.

Claire was, of course, impatient to know—and so was Karen, who had arrived in the interim, enthusiastic to know how the photo shoot had gone, and now even more enthusiastic to know why I had been taken away to assist the police in their enquiries.

"Armina Holliman is dead," I told them, flatly. "Suspicious circumstances, it seems—they wouldn't give me any details. It would hardly have been worth anyone's while to murder her, though—she was dying of cancer, with only a matter of months to live, at the most. She'd have been lucky to hold on long enough to see the exhibition."

"Why did the police want to question you?" Claire demanded.

"Because I saw her last night," I told her. "I don't think I'm a suspect. They must have tracked us down via CCTV footage of Stan More's van—the Renaissance is just up the road from the town center, which is lousy with CCTV—in which case they presumably know that we really did head eastwards again after leaving the hotel. I was back here by half past nine, and if I'm taking the right inference from what the police said, she didn't die until the early hours of the morning."

"What's the Renaissance?" Karen was quick to ask. "And who's Stan More?"

"A hotel in Reading. Stan is another of Devon Curtin's works of art: The Tree of the Knowledge of Good and Evil. He tries to live up to his image, but he's not very good at it, considering that he's had more than twenty years' practice. She phoned him—The Goddess, that is. She didn't know who else to call. The Falling Angel was there as well; her name is Kim Connor, and she's not a body-builder any more. Not in the athletic sense, anyway."

"Could this Stan have driven back there after dropping you off here?" Claire demanded.

"I suppose so. There was plenty of time. I can't see why he would, though. If he'd planned to kill her, he'd surely never have taken Kim and me to see her in the first place. Somebody else presumably knew she was back—but Melanie obviously didn't, so it can't be her private detectives, unless they're behind with their reports. Not that we can take it for granted that anyone killed her— maybe the suspicious circumstances arise from the fact that she was registered under a false name. Maybe she did just die of her cancer, or...." I didn't like to voice the suspicion that she might have committed suicide, because Karen was there, although Karen would undoubtedly have disapproved strongly of such absurd delicacy.

There was a brief pause before Claire said: "Are we in danger, Cris?"

"I can't see why we should be," I said. "We don't know anything, do we?"

"About what?" Karen asked.

"About who killed Devon Curtin."

"Did *she* know anything about that?" Claire wanted to know.

"Not that she told us," I said, wondering whether that increased or decreased the chance that we might be in danger.

"Who else did Stan with the Van tell about her being here?" This came from Karen.

"Nobody, while I was with him. After he dropped me off...well, he'll doubtless be only too eager to tell the cops if he did. He likes to have all the answers."

"And you didn't...?" Another contribution to the dual inquisition from Claire.

"No. If I'd phoned anyone, it would have been you—but it was half past nine when we got back, and I'd had a hectic day, by my standards. I was going to tell you this morning—but then Melanie turned up early, so I figured that it would be best to leave it until later. Armina had asked me to wait for a quiet moment before trying to set up a meeting between her and Melanie."

"Why did she ask you to set up a meeting?" Karen queried, in frank astonishment.

"It's complicated. She'd probably intended to ask Stan, but I probably looked better fitted for the task, incredible as that might seem to you. She and Melanie didn't get on, way back when."

"Because they were both in love with Curtin?" Claire supplied.

"I'm not sure that 'in love' is the appropriate term, but yes— they were both involved with him."

"You wouldn't be saying 'involved' if I weren't here," Karen suggested. "You mean they were both having it off with him." At least she hadn't said "fucking".

"Melanie was the jealous type, back then," I said. "She described Armina in the most uncomplimentary terms imaginable, and she was almost as rude about someone who phoned up while I was recuperating, asking to speak to Curtin. She's apparently still faithful to his memory—never married, it seems. Faithful to her art but not her clients, as she put it."

"What did you talk to The Goddess about?" Claire wanted to know.

I hesitated briefly, because of Karen's presence, but there was no way Karen was going to be excluded from the discussion now that she'd edged her way in. Rapidly, I gave both of them an abridged version of what I'd told the police.

"Cool," was Karen's enthusiastic response. "If this doesn't jerk you out of your existential stasis, Dad, nothing will. Curses and murder mysteries—it's got everything. Even literary ghosts."

"I don't like this," said Claire, in a markedly different one. "I'm beginning to wish I'd never phoned you. Getting out my forty-year old tits for you and that snidey receptionist was quite bad enough; now there's been another murder, or at least a suspicious death. All this stuff about magic and curses gives me the creeps. I had bad dreams last night, Cris—nothing new, I suppose, but...."

"I know," I said. "Me too. But there's no magic about it and there isn't any curse, even if the check has gone missing...."

I had to explain about the missing check, even though Claire had heard Melanie's initial reference to it.

"So the check with the curse on it has gone missing from the cop shop," Karen said, trying to clarify the situation in her own mind. "The check that Curtin didn't deposit, even though he didn't believe in magic…although that ought to mean, I suppose, that the curse was never activated at all. You can't deposit a twenty-year-old check, can you? The bank wouldn't accept it. So why steal it?"

"I don't know," I said, reflexively—more concerned, for the moment, with poor Claire's reaction. Had I thought about it for an instant, though, I would have probably have been able to guess exactly why it had been stolen—and by whom.

"It's bound to make the papers," Claire said, regretfully. "The connection with the murder twenty years ago will make it big news, at least locally. There really will be paparazzi after us, won't there, Cris? Is there still time to drive to Heathrow and get out, do you think?"

"It's a small world," I said. "If we run, it will only encourage them to chase us. We can just refer all enquiries to Melanie—she has the photographs now. Does she own the copyright, I wonder, or do we? We should have got her to sign a contract, shouldn't we?"

"She brought in a form while you were gone," Claire said. "It's on the kitchen table. She thought you'd have time to sign it when you came back—she wasn't expecting to get taken in for questioning herself."

I salvaged the release form and read it through. It gave Imagistic Enterprises the right to use the photographs in the exhibition, and "for publicity purposes"—which presumably meant that Melanie and Priestley could sell them to the press if they wanted to. Neither of us had signed the form, though. We could still haggle, if and when Melanie came back to pick up her car. In the meantime, the camera was still there, in its case, in a corner of the kitchen. If we wanted to, we could delete the images or download them on to my own computer. But what good would it do? Deleting them would only create a seller's market for a similar set, or anything resembling it, and taking them into my own possession would only attract even more unwanted attention.

Similar thoughts must have been running through Claire's mind. "I suppose the world's not going to go mad about a glimpse of a forty-year-old's tit," she said, mournfully. "I wish we'd got it done twenty years ago, now. We could have, couldn't we? Melanie was around then, and would have been only too eager to fill in for Curtin. I'm surprised she didn't hunt us down and insist."

"She was probably distracted," I said. "She wasn't the only one screwing her boss, but his death must have affected her like a kick in the gut—and she had all kinds of things to sort out, in practical terms. It's not surprising that we slipped through the cracks."

I glanced at Karen, realizing that I had let my language slip, but she seemed entirely oblivious to it. Her mind was elsewhere. "The check would have been traceable," she said, thoughtfully. "The police wouldn't have bothered with it twenty years ago, because they weren't interested in curses—but if it came to light now that the lady with cancer has told you about this Marley character...."

"We don't look nearly as handsome nowadays, do we," Claire observed, ruefully, still following her own train of thought. "The tattoos have aged a hell of a lot better than we have. Yours still looks good—not as big as the images in the photographs on the net, but beautifully executed: a real work of art."

"Yours too," I said, still focusing my attention on her, because she seemed troubled while Karen was anything but. "Pity about the curse." Seeing her expression, I was quick to add: "Not really. But when you think about it, not much has gone right since we got the damn things done, for either of us."

"They went a lot worse for him," she pointed out, meaning Devon Curtin.

"True. But there's still no curse. Even if one believed in such things, Karen's quite right—the check was never deposited, so the curse was never activated."

"But we don't know that for sure," Karen put in, obviously having given the matter further thought. "If the tattooist never deposited it, that might only that it was never specifically targeted, never focused....it doesn't necessarily mean that it wasn't *activated*. It might be active still—if there really were such a thing as a curse, that is."

I turned to look her in the face then, meeting her eyes without a hint of embarrassment, but with a healthy measure of parental pride. "That must be what Stanley More thinks," I said, pensively. "That's why he's so interested in everyone's dreams. He thinks—even though he doesn't quite believe in it—that the curse was misdirected, that we're all suffering because it went astray. That's why he's so interested in getting it lifted, even though he pretends that he's only curious. He's The Tree of the Knowledge of Good and Evil, after all—or thinks he is."

Are we in danger? I wondered. *How can we possibly tell?*

The doorbell rang again, sounding—just for an instant—like the knell of doom. I went to answer it, meekly, in spite of a nagging premonition of disaster. Claire and Karen could have stayed behind, but they didn't. They were fully caught up in the toils of the web now, drawn along in my wake.

We found J. K. Priestley standing on the doorstep. His grey Volvo wasn't visible, though—he must have parked it in the street, having seen that the driveway was already a trifle cluttered He seemed more than a little agitated, but he was still sufficiently intrigued to look at Claire and say: "Are you The Rose?" As soon as she nodded, however, he turned back to me. "Is Melanie still here?" he asked, anxiously, his gaze moving rapidly from side to side as Karen took up a position to my right and Claire to my left. "I need to speak with her."

"No," I said, perhaps too abruptly.

"Her car's in the driveway," the balding man pointed out.

"She's been taken to the police station," I told him. "She'll be back to collect it in due course." Reluctantly, but impelled by politeness, I said: "You can come in and wait if you like."

I expected him to jump at the chance, although I was by no means enthusiastic at the prospect, and I was quite surprised when he shook his head and turned away, without even a second lingering glance at The Rose. The news that Melanie had been taken away by the police seemed to have troubled him even further. He had taken three long strides and was well clear of the porch before I decided that I ought not to let him go. I stepped out of the porch too. Karen and Claire went with me, as if we were all tied together, fated to march in step no matter what.

"It's not about the missing check, Mr. Priestley," I called after the curator, giving my mouth permission to run away with me. "It's about Armina Holliman's death in suspicious circumstances."

The balding man stopped dead, as if he had been turned into a statue by the gorgon's glance. The paralysis lasted for a full three seconds before he slowly turned his head to face us again. He looked me in the eye, and I met the baleful stare as bravely as I could. Finally, he said: "Armina's dead?"

"So I'm told," I said, scrupulously.

"When? Where?"

"Early this morning, at a hotel in Reading." I hesitated, but couldn't help adding: "I talked to her last night."

He looked at me as if I were a scorpion that had just tumbled out of his shoe. "You?" he said. "*You* talked to her?"

"I wasn't alone," I told him. "Stanley More was there too, and Kim Connor. She called Stan because she wanted to talk to someone before letting Melanie know that she was back, and Stan picked us up on his way to see her."

"Stanley More," J. K. Priestley repeated, numbly. "And Kim Connor."

I didn't bother to fill in their titles; he had to know who they were. "It's been all go since you were last here," I informed him, equably. "Things have been moving fast."

He didn't appreciate the tone of the remark; his face was distorted by a grimace that I took to be a combination of rage and grief. He took a step toward me, and I flinched instinctively, although I didn't recoil. After all, I had reinforcements to either side. Collectively, we outnumbered him three to one—not that he showed the slightest sign of any malevolent intent.

Perhaps it was the presence of reinforcements that emboldened me. More likely it was the desire to show off in front of Karen—to show her a side of myself she'd never seen before, and make her proud of me for once.

"You're Jacob Marley, aren't you, Mr. Priestley?" I said. "Or you were. You stole the check from the evidence file when the police let you look up our names, because you were afraid that the case might become active again, and that the check's significance wouldn't be overlooked a second time—not with all the Web chat about curses, and the lunatic fringe making itself all too obvious."

He had frozen again. This time, I was the gorgon—he was looking directly at me. I had jumped to the conclusion over quite a long distance, and was exultant to discover that I'd landed dead on target.

"Armina told you," he said, jumping to a conclusion of his own. "Not that it matters, if she's dead. Not that anything matters, now."

"It matters if you're the one who shot Devon Curtin," I said, riding the wave. "It matters if the check will help convict you. It matters if you killed Armina, to shut her up."

The wrath returned to his expression and attitude in full force. "Killed Armina?" he echoed, in a tone of utter outrage. "I *loved* her, you bird-brained idiot. She's the last person in the world I would have killed."

He sounded convincing. "What about Curtin, then?" I queried, recklessly. "He was screwing her, wasn't he?"

J. K. Priestley, alias Jacob Marley, shook his head, as if he could hardly believe in the extent of my awful stupidity. "I didn't shoot Devon," he said, contemptuously. "He was an artist—and a magician, although he wouldn't admit it. I *cursed* him—in more than one way—but I didn't shoot him."

"Did he know about the drugs?" I hazarded.

"What drugs?"

"The drugs you were running under cover of Malcolm Holliman's dealings in art and antiques—the trickier part of the business."

Science progresses by trial and error; sometimes, you can learn as much from the hypotheses that fail as from those that remain unfalsified. It's perhaps as well.

"Malcolm Holliman had nothing to do with drugs," he said, still speaking contemptuously, his voice full of bile. "He was just a lawyer, organizing export permits and setting up auctions. The trickier part of the business was arranging for the export of items that didn't have permits—on behalf of the eager owners, that is. We might have been smuggling, in a technical sense, but we weren't thieves. It was just a matter of dodging red tape—although it did seem politic, as well as romantic, not to use my own name while constructing and guiding the transactions, and it was Malcolm's little joke to introduce me to his lovely wife under my pseudonym. To her, I was always 'Marley'. None of it had anything to do with drugs. What the hell do you take me for, Mr. Ellsworth?"

I knew that I'd wrecked my conclusion-jumping record irredeemably, but that didn't stop me being glib. "A Student of Magic," I said.

He expelled his breath in an expression of disgust. "So what?" he said. "It was just the power of positive thinking in a different guise. So I tried to put a curse on Devon Curtin—so what? He didn't believe in magic, or so he thought—but he didn't deposit the check, did he? When it came to the acid test, he chickened out. He couldn't maintain his unbelief in the face of the remotest possibility. He didn't deposit the check. I made my point. I had to get it back, though, when I had the chance. I'm a different man now; Jacob Marley is long dead, and I didn't want the connection being made. As I said, it was just a matter of dodging red tape—but it was against the law, and I didn't want to take any risks. I didn't think the police would notice—it was just being used as a bookmark, for God's sake."

"You're a different man, now," I said, trying to sound as if I didn't believe it. My attempt to show off in front of Karen and Claire, to play the detective and the hero, had gone awry, and I knew it. I couldn't even cut my losses by closing the door—I was out in the open, fully exposed, with Karen to my right and Claire to my left. They were only an audience of two, but they were two people in front of whom I didn't want to be made to look a fool.

"Yes," said J. K. Priestley, relentlessly. "It turned out, in the end, that I was more interested in the antiquarian aspects of magical lore than I was in its workability, and more interest in the antiquarian aspects of my exploits in chicanery than I was in the profits of deceit. When Armina ran away, I knew that I'd gone too far. I knew that I had to change. I never meant to frighten her away...."

"You didn't," I said, brutally. "She had cancer. That's why she left—to take part in some kind of clinical trial. It worked, too—except that the cancer came back...twice."

"Cancer?" He repeated, dazedly. "She left because she had cancer? *Without telling me?*"

There was nothing much to add to that. "She didn't want to," I said, moderating my tone in the direction of mild sympathy. What else could I say? Perhaps, I thought, she hadn't been entirely honest with me, or even with herself. Perhaps, deep down, she *had* been frightened. Perhaps, deep down, her unbelief in magic hadn't been able to stand up to pressure. While he'd been working on my tattoo, Devon Curtin had virtually confessed to me that his skepticism had cracked when he had been required to look a curse in the eye, although I had mistaken the confession for mere idle chitchat. The tattooist hadn't dared to deposit the check endorsed with a curse. The Goddess had run away, without telling the man who loved her that she was going, or why. If asked, Devon would doubtless have rationalized his action, just as Armina had...but at the end of the day, perhaps they simply couldn't *not* believe in magic.

Could I? I wondered. Until I faced the acid test, I wouldn't know. Even though I *knew* that there was no such thing as a curse, I wouldn't know whether I could avoid belief until I actually had to make a decision in which that knowledge came into conflict with the neurological disposition to believe.

J. K. Priestley looked as if he might be about to faint. "May I change my mind and come inside for a few minutes, Mr. Ellsworthy?" he said.

The polite thing to do would have been to say yes immediately. The generous and merciful thing to do would have been to offer him a cup of tea, sit him down, and commiserate with him over the loss of the love that he had lost, twenty years before. Chivalry demanded no less—and yet, I hesitated.

He who hesitates is rarely lost, I had once been wont to say, provided that he uses the margin of hesitation constructively. I wish I had used that moment of unwonted hesitation constructively. I wish, in fact, that there had been a constructive way in which I might have been able to use the margin in question. There wasn't. I just hesitated, as was always my habit, my reflex, while Karen and Claire stood to either side of me, meekly waiting for me to do the right thing.

And J. K. Priestley just stood there too, waiting for me to make up my mind.

He was still standing there when someone shot him in the back and he collapsed at my feet, as good as dead before he hit the ground.

CHAPTER THIRTEEN

When someone gets shot in the back in a movie, and the camera slowly pans around to reveal the shooter, you expect to see a tall, lean professional assassin in black hat, with a sneer on his face, or a scorned wife playing the fury whose like is unknown in Hell. You don't expect to see a clinically-obese ex-bodybuilder with a wondrously child-like face temporarily twisted into an expression of disgust.

I'd like to be able to say that she had appeared as if by magic, but there was nothing magical about it. My direly unkempt garden had given her all the cover she'd needed to approach us unseen, in spite of her bulk. The bindweed-covered bushes could have hidden a rhinoceros, if not an elephant.

How long she'd been lurking there I had no idea, but I deduced that the attention she had paid to our conversation had been a trifle selective. She'd had preconceived ideas of her own, through which the information had filtered.

She was holding the pistol with practiced firmness and determination. Obviously body-building hadn't been the only unusual hobby she'd had twenty-some years before. Just as obviously, she hadn't surrendered her handgun when it became illegal to keep one.

"It's all his fault," said Kim Connor, The Falling Angel. "It's all his fault."

I knew what the "all" in question was. Kim Connor believed—or, at least, couldn't *not* believe—that she had been cursed, twenty years before. Thanks to Armina Holliman, she now knew the exact words of the curse. *May all the troubles of this world descend upon you, and may the anticipation of your allotted place in Hell echo in your living soul.* She hadn't reacted with any undue violence at the time, but that was because the words had needed time to settle in her flesh, and the meaning to settle in her consciousness. There was no doubt, now, that the anticipation of her allotted place in Hell was echoing in her living soul

She had felt the effects of that curse for twenty years: the curse that Devon Curtin had refrained from bringing down specifically upon himself; the curse that the tattooist had, instead, used as a bookmark in his account-book, from which position—according to Kim's diagnosis—it had been free to infect all of his clients. It had, in fact, been sitting in that ledger for twenty years, quietly working its magic.

Except that there was no magic, really. There was no curse. Kim's bad dreams and personal misfortunes, like everyone else's were perfectly natural. How could she bring herself to believe that, though? How could she ever have believed it, given that she was in Stanley More's little discussion-cum-therapy group, given that she had gone to Devon Curtin in the first place, as a body-builder ambitious to show herself off to glorious advantage, and had gladly consented to host The Falling Angel, on his way to demonhood, and to accept him as her *animus*? How could she ever have believed, even for a moment, that there was no magic in the world?

I looked around, at the three rows of semi-detached houses whose back gardens surrounded the patch of land where my own house stood. Surely, I thought, someone must have heard the pistol shot. Someone must have recognized it for what it was. Someone must even now be telling the 999 operator that armed police were urgently needed at my address.

In Maidenhead? Who the hell was I kidding?

I knew that Karen and Claire were still beside me, one to my right and the other to me left. Neither of them had moved an inch. They were too frightened to reach for their mobile phones and dial 999 while Kim Connor's gun was pointing at me, as it now was. Her hand seemed perfectly steady and purposeful, but that didn't mean that she wasn't crazy enough to shoot—all three of us, if the whim took her—and she had time and bullets enough to do it

I finally knew the answer to the question of whether we were in danger.

I guessed, very belatedly, who it was that Melanie Millward had been talking to on the phone on the evening when I became The Nightingale—the "groupie" whose message she had promised to pass on, without ever intending to. Melanie had, after all, meant "reeking of steroids", not "reeking of pheromones", even though it didn't really make sense.

I still wasn't frightened for myself, even though the gun was aimed at my heart. I was only frightened for Karen and Claire. Reflexively, I put out my arms as if I could somehow shield them both.

"Hello, Kim," I said. "That probably wasn't a wise move. The police will be bringing Melanie back from the station at any moment. You might have got away with shooting Devon Curtin twenty years ago, but you're not going to get away with this one."

"That should have worked," Kim said, earnestly. "Killing Devon should have lifted the curse—but it didn't. It's all *his* fault." She flicked a glance at J. K. Priestley's prone body, but the gun never wavered.

"But the curse has been lifted now," I hastened to say. "He retrieved the check from the ledger. It's over."

It seemed like a neat move, but it didn't work. "No it isn't," she retorted. "The dreams haven't gone away. There's only one way to make them go away."

There were no prizes for guessing what she meant, after the previous night's conversation.

"Why on Earth did you shoot Armina?" I asked. "It certainly wasn't her fault."

She stared at me, her child-like face suddenly overwhelmed by apparent innocence. "I didn't shoot Armina," she said, her slightly-injured tone utterly convincing. Unfortunately, she spoiled the effect by adding: "I just cuddled her until she went to sleep. I couldn't stand to see her suffer. If that was what the curse had done to her, I thought, what was it going to do to the rest of us, given time? I knew I had to do something. I knew that it couldn't go on. Now it's your turn."

"I know what I have to do," I said, hastily. "You have my word that I'll take care of it—that *we*'ll take care of it." The arm that I'd placed in front of Claire went to her shoulder, as if by its own volition, to indicate that she was included in the *we*. You can trust us, Kim," I continued. "We'll see to it that the curse is lifted."

"Bloody hell, Dad!" Karen whispered. I didn't dare make any response.

It was Kim's turn to hesitate.

"You don't actually want to watch us, do you?" I said, feeling fairly sure that she didn't. It wasn't, however, a matter of wanting—not, at least, of Kim's wanting. Kim was in conflict with herself, with The Falling Angel. The bells of Hell were echoing in her soul, and she was already lost and damned, all hope abandoned even if she wasn't quite ready to face up to the fact. She wasn't about to turn around meekly and go home, trusting to my word that Claire and I would take care of everything.

I could hardly blame her. After all, we couldn't, could we?

J. K. Priestley was lying at my feet, the impact of the bullet having thrust him forwards so that his head was practically touching my toes. His arms were spread out, like extended wings. He was still bleeding, but not moving, still alive but never going to regain consciousness.

"Please lower the gun, Kim," I said, gently. "After all, you don't want to hurt any of us. We're the last people in the world you want to hurt. You need us, if the curse is to be lifted."

"You said last night that it was too late," she said, although she clearly didn't want to believe it, and probably couldn't.

"But Armina pointed out that I was mistaken," I countered. "We're not talking about a mere matter of visual art, are we? We're talking about magic. It's not too late, Kim. We have time. Please lower the gun."

She seemed reassured. She tried to smile. But she didn't lower the gun. Her consciousness and her autonomic nervous system were still in conflict. Her neurological disposition was screwing things up, even though her name was short of a y, and her consciousness short of a why. There was something in her that was ready to shoot, even though I was the last person in the world she wanted to kill. There was something in her that was beyond the reach of all her conscious arguments, however reasonable or crazy they might be. The Falling Angel hadn't reached rock bottom after all, He was still in the game. I was still in danger.

"Please, Kim," I said, as soothingly as I could. "I thought you liked me. Last night, in Stan's van, there was a connection, wasn't there—a spark?"

"But you didn't like me," she retorted, with all-too-deadly accuracy. I knew that if she fired the gun, the bullet would strike me in the heart. She wouldn't miss. And then....

I felt Karen close beside me, tacitly clinging to me in fear, looking to me for rescue, for succor. But what could I do? I couldn't work magic.

"I couldn't respond because I love Claire," I said, as soothingly as anyone could. "I need to love Claire, don't I? If I didn't, I couldn't lift the curse. *You* need me to love Claire."

She was still hesitating—but mere hesitation, I realized, wasn't going to be enough. Even if the police car brought Melanie back to collect her Citroen, that wouldn't make the situation any better, and almost certainly worse. If the cavalry were to arrive, it had to be something better than a W.P.C. and a C.S.O.—and it certainly wouldn't be a good idea for Melanie Millward to appear on the scene, because I was perfectly certain that Kim wouldn't have forgotten that telephone conversation on the eve of the murder, even though it had been twenty years ago.

The time for hesitation was over. I stepped forward, over J. K. Priestley's body, and positioned myself between the barrel of the gun and Karen. I felt that I was letting Claire down by leaving her exposed, but what could I do? I wasn't entirely certain that a bullet fired at me wouldn't pass clean through me and kill Karen too, but the bullet that had struck J. K. Priestley down couldn't have gone right through him, or it would have hit me. What else could I do?

I stretched out my right hand. "Let me take the gun, Kim," I said. "You don't need it any more. It's all up to me now. I'll take care of everything."

She didn't surrender the gun. I looked into her eyes, sternly and steadily, and I saw that she wasn't going to surrender the gun. There was something in her that wouldn't let her, something that didn't care about *her* in the least, something that wanted her damnation to continue to the bitter end. She was locked into a bad dream, beyond the reach of everyday logic, even though she was still debating with herself, still trying to reason a way through,

All people with tattoos are possessed, Stanley More had said, one way or another. Some are possessed by plaintive birds, some by angels *en route* to demonhood, and some by other songs, other fears, other attempts to command or summon fate.

Shit, I thought, hoping that Karen, at least, might have time enough, and ingenuity enough, to make her escape if and when the aforementioned shit hit the fan.

I was almost reconciled to being shot, to taking a bullet in the hope that Karen and Claire might be able to escape thereafter—and then I heard the cavalry coming, bang on cue, in the nick of time.

Kim heard it too, and undoubtedly recognized the sound: the growl of the engine of Stanley More's ancient van, as it juddered to a halt behind the red Citroen.

Kim didn't turn round, but she was probably as sharply aware as I was of Stanley More stepping down from the van and slamming the door. He was alone, but he was armed—with a spade.

I didn't suppose for a moment that he had come to keep his promise to put my ill-kept garden in order at a generous discount. It was more likely by far that he had been impelled by burning curiosity. He had come to ask me how the photo-shoot had gone, and what I had said to Melanie about Armina, and what Melanie had said to me…and a hundred other things that The Tree of the Knowledge of Good and Evil really needed to know, if he were to keep up appearances.

  Whatever the reason for his opportune appearance, however, he had seen Kim standing at the end of the driveway, pointing a gun at my heart, and J. K. Priestley lying dead on the doorstep. Being the man he was, he hadn't picked up his mobile phone to call for help. He had picked up his spade in order to bring it in person. Kim was his friend, after all. He was party to her nightmares.

"Hello, Stan," I said, as he approached along the driveway. "We've had a little trouble, I fear. Kim's a bit upset."

"Put the gun down, Kim," Stan said, addressing the back of her head because she still hadn't turned around. "You don't want to hurt him—we need him. It's not just you, you know—we *all* need him."

She relaxed, just a little. "It was *his* fault, Stan," she said, meaning J. K. Priestley. "It was all his fault."

"No it wasn't," said Stan. "He was just some wanker playing mind games. He didn't know what he was doing any more than Devon did. But we know the truth. We know what we're doing— and we need The Nightingale and the Rose. We have to let them take over now, to do what needs to be done."

"We can't trust them," Kim said. "You know that."

"We don't need to trust them," he replied. "We just have to let nature take its course. They have their parts to play—trust doesn't come into it."

He was right. She probably trusted him, thanks to the pressure of long habit—but trust didn't come into it. He wasn't about to take any chances. The moment she began to turn around to look him in the eye, and the gun was no longer pointing at anyone's heart, he smashed her over the head with the spade.

She collapsed in an ungainly heap. The gun didn't go off.

Stan looked down at her pityingly, and I knew that he was hoping with all his heart that she wasn't dead. "Silly cunt," he said. "She was only supposed to keep watch, while I was at the cop shop. She wasn't supposed to have a gun, let alone to use it. To think that I never figured it out. We've only been swapping our nightmares for twenty fucking years. It was right under my nose. I should have figured it out. Some fucking Tree of Knowledge I am."

"Mind your language, Stan," I objected. "The Rose is right here—and this is my daughter." Karen wasn't interested in introductions, though. She had flung her arms around my neck, and was sobbing with relief. Even Claire had clutched my arm, convulsively. I didn't mind either contact in the least; I was as much in need of comfort as they were, and my ANS knew it.

"There, there," I said, for lack of anything more constructive to say, as I hesitantly returned Karen's embrace, and moved a little closer to Claire. "There, there."

CHAPTER FOURTEEN

"Try not to come back here quite so soon," D.S. Williamson said to me, when my second interview of the day was finally concluded. "It's not that we have anything against you personally, but you seem to be a bit of a Jonah."

It would have been pointless to explain to him that I couldn't be "a bit of a Jonah" because there was no such thing, that the merest glance at my life-history would prove that my ability to make things happen was, in fact, distinctly under par, and that the implication that I might be some sort of fatal catalyst was plainly nonsensical, so I kept my mouth shut.

I continued to keep it shut when I reached the outer office of the police station, where Melanie Millward and Claire were waiting for me. Karen, alas, had already been whisked off to Bracknell by her mother, who had been obliged to pretend to be a responsible adult in order to accompany Karen in her interview. The first thing anyone said to me was: "Thanks to your big mouth, I'm down one exhibition curator." It was, of course, Melanie who said it.

There were so many things I could have said in reply. I might even have ventured the opinion that if it hadn't been for her ill-use of her own big mouth, including keeping it shut when a distraught and steroid-addled Kim Connor had asked her to make sure that Devon Curtin returned her phone call, the whole tragedy might have been averted. Chivalry demanded, however, that I maintain a diplomatic silence, and try not to feel overly offended.

The reason that Melanie and Claire were waiting for me turned out to have nothing to do with any desire to hail me as a hero, and everything to do with the fact that W.P.C. only wanted to make one trip when she drove us all back to my house. Not that I would be allowed into my house, given that it was a crime scene, but the red Citroen and the yellow Datsun were still there, sufficiently far away from the spot marked X for the police to agree that they could be driven away. While I'd been otherwise occupied, Melanie and Claire had agreed among themselves, and with W.P.C. Craig, that Claire would put me up for the night in Farnham.

I didn't even pause to wonder whether Melanie had fought Claire for the privilege of letting me stay over while I wasn't allowed back into my own house, because I knew full well that she hadn't. Melanie didn't believe in magic and more than Devon Curtin or Stanley More, but she was just as interested, if only for reasons of curiosity and completing a good story, in "letting nature take its course". Like Devon and Stan, she figured that she knew exactly which course nature would run. Personally, I wasn't so sure.

"You didn't have to do that," I said to Claire, gratefully.

"Well, it didn't look as if your ex-wife was about to make the offer," Claire replied, evidently having crossed paths with Liz somewhere in the course of recent events. "I backed your daughter up when she tried to tell her mother how brave you'd been, and how you might have saved our lives, given that the crazy lady could easily have gone off on a Cumbrian spree, but your ex wouldn't listen. All she could see was that you'd been the one who'd put her beloved daughter in harm's way. Karen wasn't even supposed to be at your place, apparently."

I sighed. "Well," I admitted, "the one thing of which I could never accuse Liz is not being fond of my daughter." I turned to Melanie then. "I seriously doubt that exhibition curators are a dime a dozen," I said, "but I'd be willing to bet that they flock to publicity of the sort you're going to get like flies to horseshit. You'll be okay. Have the police promised to release your digital camera a little more quickly than your old appointment-book?"

"Oh yes," she said. "This case is already closed—and so is the other one, it's rumored, thanks to the elaborate confession Kim Connor made when she recovered from the blow on the head. She didn't even wait to get into the interview room before blurting it all out, apparently. She's back on the steroids, you know—hoped that it might help her look thinner by turning her fat to muscle. They were always more likely to kill her by overburdening her heart and arteries—but not quite quickly enough to save Armina and Jakey from her diabolical wrath."

"It wasn't diabolical wrath that led her to kill Armina," I corrected her. "More like angelic tenderness. She was a creature of contradictions."

"Aren't we all?" Melanie replied, far too glibly. "Most of us, fortunately, can live with our contradictions, or Broadmoor would be bursting at the seams." She turned her head to look at W.P.C. Craig, who was ready to drive and keen to clear us out of the station. "She *will* end up in Broadmoor rather than Holloway, won't she?"

"Probably," said the policewoman. "I can't imagine why the C.P.S. would want to try her for murder, given that she's obviously off her head. In my book, mind, anyone who gets themselves tattooed is off her head. Why pay someone to stick needles in you for hours on end, at God-knows-how-many stabs per second?"

I expected Melanie to react hotly to that one, but she was busy clambering into the back of the police car. I wasn't at all sure that I was the right person to defend the case, but chivalry seemed to demand it, on Claire's behalf if not Melanie's. Besides which, everyone seemed to be assuming that I would take the front seat, so it was obviously my job to ride shotgun.

"It's painful," I said, "and there's a danger of infection if it's not done right, but there's no lack of sanity about it, because the potential rewards outweigh the pain and the risk."

"What rewards?" the skeptical policewoman demanded. "Giving your fellow men something to laugh at, and making them think that you're a prat?"

I was willing to bet that there were plenty of tattoos on display at changing time in the police locker rooms, male and female alike, but that wasn't much of a line of attack. "It's not really a matter of showing off to other people," I said. "Most tattoos remain secret, most of the time, because of the way they're situated and the human habit of wearing clothes. The real ideal observer of a tattoo is the mind's own eye—which sees just as well if the tattoo is at the base of your spine as it does if it's blazoned across your chest. It's a matter of self-transformative magic—and although the magic in question is all in the mind, more metaphorical than literal, the opposition between the two concepts is more of a continuum than a matter of either/or. You are what you pretend to be, so you have to be careful what you pretend to be—but you have to pretend as hard as you can, if you want to be anything at all. Tattoos are aids to pretence, and should be respected rather than scorned on that account."

The policewoman didn't put up an elaborate argument, but it wasn't a long drive back to my house—not, at least, the way W.P.C. Craig drove, which was based on the assumption that all other road users would get the hell out of her way if they saw a police car coming towards them.

The W.P.C. didn't get out of the car when she dropped us off. She was in a hurry to get on with things. She'd had a busy day.

We had to walk past the Citroen to get to the Datsun, so Melanie was the first to peel off from our little party. "Have a good night," she said to us, not trying overly hard to suppress a lewd smirk. "Sweet dreams."

"You too," said Claire, through slightly gritted teeth. "But then, I don't suppose you ever have nightmares, do you?"

"Not often," Melanie retorted, defiantly—and surely not entirely honestly, given that she probably wasn't the kind of person fortunate enough to forget her dreams as soon as she woke up, if not before. "You really ought to reconsider the possibility of appearing live in the exhibition, you know. Now that circumstances have brought you together again, you'd be fools not to make the most of it."

"But we are fools," I said. I didn't add that love—or lust—makes fools of us all, perpetually steering us in directions that are as likely to be wrong as right, as likely to be crazy as sane, precisely because of its magical ability to break the normal chains of cause and effect. I'd only been grandstanding when I'd told Kim Connor that I loved Claire, but it was true. I'd loved her twenty years ago and had never really buried or masked that love completely, no matter what had happened in the interim—which didn't diminish what I'd once felt for Liz, and still felt for Karen, in the least.

Claire's house in Farnham turned out to be a thoroughly modern pocket-sized semi, with a through lounge, a tiny bathroom and only two bedrooms. By comparison with my place, it seemed claustrophobic, although Claire presumably preferred to think of it as cozy.

"You can have Peter's old room," Claire told me. It was the first time she'd spoken her dead son's name in my presence. I still didn't know her current surname. "It's okay. I haven't kept it just the way it was, as a shrine to his memory. It's just a room—a spare room."

"Thanks," I said.

"I don't feel like cooking," she said. "Shall we just order a pizza?"

"Fine by me," I said.

"I need a drink, though. Red wine okay? It's nothing fancy—South African, I think."

"Fine by me," I repeated.

The conversation ran along much the same lines for some time, always trivial, never giving rise to the slightest hint of disagreement. We were strangers, after all. Even our twenty-year-old selves had never really got to know one another, and I was wary of asking her too many questions about her life in the interim, in case I touched any elephantine sore spots, which would obviously have been far too easy to do. We both found it easier to talk about Katla than Kim Connor, and the budget deficit rather than the art of tattooing.

Eventually, though, we had to go to bed. I asked Claire whether she kept a spare toothbrush for emergencies. She did.

I would have left it at that, figuring that there was all the time in the world to make progress, if there were any progress to be made. She was the one whose autonomic nervous system was wired up the common-or-garden way. She was the one who naturally looked people in the eye, and didn't shy away from the slightest touch.

"Just because people expect it of us," she said, "it doesn't mean that we have to live up to their expectations. They're all crazy, when all's said and done. You and I don't believe in magic. There isn't a curse, so it doesn't need lifting. There's no magic in the tattoos that could possibly require completion."

"I know," I said. "Just because our neurological dispositions make it so hard to refuse belief in magic, it doesn't mean that we oughtn't to do our utmost to hold fast to the principles of science. After all, it's just a matter of maintaining consciousness, of concentrating on the truth."

"And we have free will," she continued. "It's not as if we're prisoners of fate, bound to fulfill the universe's intentions. We can choose. We can do anything we want to do, for whatever motives we care to act upon, and we don't have to do anything that we don't want to do."

"Better than that," I said. "We're free to indulge the imp of the perverse, and do anything at all without any motive at all, just for the hell of it." It wasn't the unquiet spirit of Edgar Allan Poe speaking—just me. Whoever the ghost in question was haunting nowadays, it had to be someone far more capable of art-work than me. Needless to say I didn't dare protest that the *thing* in question wasn't something I didn't want to do. "We're the masters of our own destiny," I rambled on, "and there's nothing else at stake. We know perfectly well that whatever we do, in private and in secret, is incapable of having any effect whatsoever on the world at large. We have no responsibility to anyone but ourselves, and what we choose to do is no one's business but our own."

It was all true—every single word. Confining human life to the truth isn't easy, though. We have a neurological disposition to lie.

Anyway, we'd had a hard day, in the course of which our nervous systems had been raised to fever pitch more than once. Excitement of the nervous system is psychologically negotiable. The sensation of being stung by needles can be renegotiated into lust, if one has the knack of so doing.

"There's just one thing," I said, bravely, when Claire didn't seem capable of taking up the thread, "that we ought perhaps to consider—one simple thing that really would give us the opportunity to make a gesture, to exercise our own idiosyncratic influence on the pressure and course of fate. We could do it for ourselves, first of all, and then, perhaps, for anyone else who might be caught up in the pattern, whether by circumstance, belief or simply the failure to suspend belief."

"What's that?" she asked.

I explained.

She agreed.
We did it.

EPILOGUE

CONNUBIAL BLISS

That night, I dreamed a story about a nightingale, a needle and a rose, although I'm not quite sure whether I dreamed it while I was asleep or awake, and perfectly certain that it doesn't matter. The story itself took time to coalesce, for there was a prelude in which many nightingales were featured, and many needles too, and far more than one rose. In the prelude, there were needles that suppressed pain and needles that stimulated it, nightingales that played the saint and nightingales that played the sinner, roses that were blood red and roses that were snow white, but as the climax of the dream new nearer all the nightingales became one, all the needles became one, and all the roses faded briefly into the background.

The nightingale that emerged as the protagonist of the dream, whose name was Luscinia, had had the misfortune to annoy a witch with her nocturnal singing—or perhaps a wizard, given that such things can remain confused in dreams. The word "witch" should not, in any case, be restricted to individuals of the female sex any more than the word "nightingale" should. Perhaps it was actually *his* singing that annoyed *him*, for reality can sometimes intrude into dreams as a confusing factor, but in stories, as a rule, both nightingales and witches are females, and it is never wise to disobey rules in stories.

Why was the witch annoyed? Who knows? Perhaps she was hypersensitive. Witches are traditionally cursed with irritability, and the impulse to punish. The simple fact is that singing of the nightingale Luscinia annoyed her, probably because it was too beautiful and too plaintive, and so she trapped the bird, and ran red-hot needles into the poor creature's frightened eyes, so that Luscinia would no longer know when night had fallen and that it was time to sing. In addition to that, she cursed the singer's voice, ordaining that henceforth, the voice of the nightingale would cause pain to anyone who heard it, in spite of its beautiful and plaintive qualities.

Not unnaturally, Luscinia was hurt herself by this punishment, because she loved to sing, but hated to cause pain. Sometimes, she remained silent for long periods of time—years, or even decades—because she did not want to cause pain to those who heard her singing. Sometimes, however, she would be unable to contain herself any longer, and she would give voice, by night or by day—because she could no longer tell the difference—in spite of her merciful inclinations. In order to share the martyrdom of her listeners, however, Luscinia always pressed herself against a needle-sharp thorn while she sang, and drove the point of the thorn more deeply into her own flesh as she sang more loudly or for longer periods of time. She hurt herself badly by so doing, but the tip of the thorn never penetrated her heart, because the witch's curse would not allow that.

Eventually, sickened by her plight, the nightingale flew to the tree of the knowledge of good and evil, which had the reputation of being able to answer any question correctly, though not necessarily wisely. Luscinia asked the tree what she must do to lift the witch's curse—or, alternatively, to force the needle-like thorn to penetrate her heart in order that she might die, forsaking the torment of her irrepressible desire to sing.

"There is only one way to break the witch's curse," the tree told her, "and there are no alternatives involved. You already know what it is that you must do to lift the curse. You do, indeed, have to let the blood flow out of your heart, and the song from your soul, but you cannot do that alone. In order to persuade the thorny needle to complete its work you must provide a receptacle into which the blood might flow, and that receptacle must be the corolla of a white rose. Nor will any rose suffice, for you must find a rose which desires, more fervently than anything else in the world, to be red."

At first, this did not seem too difficult a task to Luscinia, for the world was full of roses of every color imaginable, and she could not believe that there was no rose among them which did not envy the color of another. She began to question white roses, to determine which among them yearned to be red.

Alas, there was none! Every white rose in the world, it seemed, had no desire to be other than white, and every one of them said that even if it were to become discontented with its purity, the last color in the world it would want to be was the red of human blood. For years, and then for decades, the nightingale pursued her futile quest. Occasionally, while she did so, she could not help yielding to the pressure of her nature and giving voice, knowing as she did so that she was causing pain to anyone who might hear her. She always pressed her breast to a needle-sharp thorn as she did so, but the thorn would never puncture her heart, in order to let her life's blood flow away.

That quest might have gone on forever, had Luscinia only had the advice of the tree of the knowledge of good and evil to draw upon in opposing the witch's curse—as might have been the case, had she been more respectful of the rules of magic and storytelling. In the end, however, she decided that, if the formula that had been prescribed to her was impossible to put into operation, then she must take the risk of varying it, according to her own inclination, her own whim and her own enterprise.

Having come to this decision, Luscinia began to search, not among white roses for one that yearned to be red, but among red roses for one that yearned to be white. That was not easy either; no matter how abhorrent white roses found the idea of being stained the color of human blood, the vast majority of blood-red roses seemed quite content with their condition, and had no desire to be purified.

In the end, though, after years of searching, Luscinia found a red rose that yearned to be white.

"This is what we must do," said the nightingale to the red rose. "You must position yourself above me, while I lay still amid the thorny branches of your tree, and I will sing a very special song of pain and sorrow. You must be strong, and brave, for my song will hurt you more than you can possibly anticipate, but if you can steel yourself against the effects of the witch's curse, the color will begin to flow out of your petals and fall, one drop at a time, on to my breast. Then the hollow thorn will allow it to pass into the chambers of my heart, which will drink it in. There, your color will fill me more abundantly with life than I have ever been filled before, and my song will be transformed. It will still be beautiful, and plaintive, but it will be a song of love, and not of pain."

So that is what the rose and the nightingale did—and the experience was incredibly sharp, more intense than anything either of them had ever experienced before, or thought possible. The rose was strong enough and brave enough, however, while the nightingale was capable of holding so much life, that the magic was complete, and the conclusion a happy one.

The witch's curse was turned back upon itself, and everyone else lived a little less unhappily for ever afterwards…which is how stories are supposed to end, according to the rules. If they didn't end that way, their magic wouldn't work, and might even turn black.

Had I been a pilgrim making progress I would doubtless have woken up and beheld that it was a dream, but I wasn't conscious of any such awakening or any such beholding. All I know for sure is that Devon Curtin's work of art and magic spell—if there ever was a magic component to his artistry in any but a purely metaphorical sense—was finally activated, although not quite as he had envisaged it. We turned it around, just for the hell of it. And so absorbed were we in what we were doing that it did not seem to us that we were turning our own position upside-down at all, but that we remained exactly as we were, and had always been, and had always been meant to be, while the world around us turned upside down, and was finally set to rights after spinning topsy-turvy through half an eternity.

It was just a crazy fancy, mind. If the world really had been turned upside-down, its overturned inhabitants were blissfully unaware of the fact, and went on with their topsy-turvy adventures exactly as before, or very nearly so.

That's often the way when dreams dissolve and stories end, isn't it? Nothing seems to have changed in reality, and any pleasant residue of feeling remaining from the product of the imagination quickly comes to seem delusory, its magic dispelled. That doesn't mean, however, that dreams are not worthwhile, or that they're not magical. We are what we pretend to be, so we must pretend, as forcefully and as cleverly as we can, to be what we truly want and need to be—no matter how awkwardly our innate neurological dispositions might strive to inhibit us in our quest.

ABOUT THE AUTHOR

BRIAN STABLEFORD was born in Shipley, Yorkshire, in 1948. He spent most of his working life as a full-time writer, although he taught various subjects for brief periods at the University of Reading, the University of the West of England and what is now the University of Winchester. He has published more than seventy novels, most notably *The Empire of Fear, Year Zero, The Fountains of Youth, The Stones of Camelot, Alien Abduction: The Wiltshire Revelations* and *Prelude to Eternity*, and more than twenty short story collections, including several volumes of "tales of the biotech revolution". His non-fiction books include *Scientific Romance in Britain: 1890-1950, Glorious Perversity: The Decline and Fall of Literary Decadence, Science Fact and Science Fiction: An Encyclopedia* and *The Devil's Party: A Brief History of Satanic Abuse*. Since being relegated from the commercial arena to hobbyist work in the small press field he has translated more than fifty volumes of classic crime fiction and scientific romance from the French, including a five-volume set of the scientific marvel fiction of Maurice Renard, and a six-volume set of scientific romances by J. H. Rosny the Elder. He lives with his elderly mother in Hadleigh, Essex.

www.ingramcontent.com/pod-product-compliance
Lightning Source LLC
Chambersburg PA
CBHW022153260626
47155CB00018B/1868